Daughter of Rising Moon

Portrait of a Potawatomi Storyteller

To Erin, Jay, Elese, Katherine, Jenna and Michael —
with all good wishes —

by William Barnaby Faherty, S.J.

Father Faherty S.J.

Copyright © 2007, Fr. William Barnaby Faherty, S.J.
All rights reserved.

Published in cooperation with

Reedy Press
PO Box 5131
St. Louis, MO 63139
USA

No part of this publication may be reproduced or transmitted in any form or by any means, electronic or mechanical, including photocopy, recording, or any information storage and retrieval system, without permission in writing from the publisher.

Permissions may be sought directly from Reedy Press at the above mailing address or via our website at www.reedypress.com.

Library of Congress Control Number: 2007938709

ISBN: 978-0-9800475-1-6

For information on all Reedy Press publications visit our website at www.reedypress.com.

Printed in the United States of America
07 08 09 10 11 5 4 3 2 1

Cover image: *Clara Singer, Navajo Grandmother*, by Edward Carno, 1978, courtesy The St. Stanislaus Historical Museum Society, Inc.

Contents

I. Orion Ruhane: An Irish Potwatomi   1
   A. A Lecturer Lights a Fire (1992)   2
   B. Emily Rising Moon   9

II. The Story of the "True People"   15
   A. The Neshnabek (1600)   16
   B. The Coming of the French (1650)   26
   C. The Powerful Potawatomi (1765–1830)   33
   D. Kansas-Bound (1830–1860)   40

III. Family Backgrounds   50
   A. Out of Ruma (1878)   51
   B. "Father Butler's Boys"   56

IV. Orion Grows Up   62
   A. St. Mary's, Kansas (1944)   63
   B. Post-War Kansas (1945)   69
   C. St. Mary's High School (1946–1947)   76
   D. Interlude at Oskaloosa   81
   E. Senior Classman (1952)   92

V. Different Horizon   97
   A. The Birthplace of the Blackrobes   98

Author's Note   107

DEDICATED TO:

Deacon William Eugene Kessler

and his son

Father William Eugene Kessler, Jr.

I

Orion Ruhane

An Irish Potawatomi

A

A Lecturer Lights a Fire

Orion Ruhane had trouble giving his full attention to the speaker at the University of New Mexico. Orion had driven down to Albuquerque from Denver, where he was a Jesuit professor of history at Regis College, to hear talks on the literature of New Mexico. Southwestern writers had always fascinated him, and he wanted to learn more about them. Instead, an unscheduled lecturer was giving his own highly personalized view of the literature of the American Indian.

Orion had no objections to Indians or their writings. In spite of his Gaelic name and a face that many thought typically Irish, he was part Indian and a writer himself. Both his grandmothers belonged to the Neshnabek, the "True People," or, as the white people mistakenly called them, the Potawatomi, the "People of the Fire." Orion published stories and a newspaper column called "Brightside."

He couldn't stomach Whites who appointed themselves defenders of the Tribes without fully understanding the views of those they tried to defend. The Columbian Quincentennial had brought painful memories to his people, and such Whites were not healing wounds.

The speaker had talked first of Scott Momaday's prize-winning novel *House Made of Dawn*. Orion had never been able to get far into that book. He had liked the title but little else. Momaday had done much better, Orion thought, on his shorter work, *The Way to Rainy Mountain*. That book could have won the Pulitzer, in Orion's view.

The lecturer told of his own meetings with the prize-winning author. On one occasion, he had told Momaday that he wrote better than Michener. The writer had assured the lecturer that he appreciated his perceptivity. Orion thought of Michener's regional books such as *Centennial* and *Hawaii* and of Momaday's *House Made of Dawn*. He wondered why anyone would try to compare unlike things or writers with differing approaches.

At the end of the lecture, no one ventured a question. Orion raised his hand. When recognized, he said, "I could not get in the front door of *House Made of Dawn*."

"Lots of white people face that problem," the speaker said sharply. His defensive tone suggested that he'd welcome no more questions.

Orion muttered to himself, "Some Indians might have that problem, too."

The assembled adults gradually headed for the student dining hall two buildings away.

That evening, the director of the program invited all the participants to his home for "decaf and literary conversation." Orion drove one-third of the way up Sandia Mountain to the director's residence. It gave a thrilling view of the city of Albuquerque below. The aroma of evergreens filled the clear air. A bird feeder filled with honey water brought the greatest bevy of hummingbirds Orion had ever seen. The heat of the day had left with the setting sun.

"Will we hear a little about other writers tomorrow—the poets and the essayists?" Orion asked his host. "Perhaps Ramona Cardin. I met her on a Frontier plane going to Gallup some years ago."

"I would hope so," the director answered.

The lecturer did not meet the director's and Orion's hopes the next morning. He talked about his youthful experiences on the Navajo reservation as the son of a white trader. On a visit to the reservation some years before, Orion had wondered at first why anyone who did not have to would choose to live in such a remote place. But when he learned the financial return from a trading post, he no longer wondered.

As most outsiders who study the Diné, as the Navajo called themselves, Orion had come to admire them greatly. He thought a perfect description of the people came in Willa Cather's *Death Comes for the Archbishop*. The New Mexico prelate spoke of the Navajo as "a people with an edge." They certainly differed from his own people, both in looks and in outlook. Their marriage customs intrigued Orion. Often in sermons he contrasted the Navajo procedures with the current American practice that anthropologist Margaret Mead called the worst ever conceived by any society.

The lecturer continued with his own personal impressions of the Diné. None of his hearers had any questions. He devoted Wednesday's lecture to unwritten legends of the Navajo but nothing of the poetry or short stories by other members of the Diné or by members of other tribes.

By Thursday, the speaker had turned from the good Indian to the bad white man. Berating his fellow Caucasians seemed to be his penance for ancestral sins against the tribes. Orion simply refused to welcome a white man's berating of his fellows. That trend, he felt, moved in the wrong direction. He closed his mind so he would not be tempted to open his mouth. He simply began to consider what he would say in his next Sunday's sermon.

During his seminary course on the way to becoming a priest, Orion had given extra attention to colonial mission history. He learned the doctrine of Paul, Augustine, and Aquinas. But he also knew of Kino and Marquette, the missionary explorers. The Whites had often treated the Indians harshly, but the street ran two ways. The Iroquois harassed the Hurons and the white man. By the time

Columbus reached San Salvador, the Caribs had come out of the Orinoco Valley on the north coast of South America and had conquered the peoples in many of the islands that came to bear their name. They took no prisoners when they fought natives or Europeans.

The lecturer drifted into the religion of the Indians. He described the Navajo Prayer for rain: male rain with thunder and lightning; female rain with a steady pour that brought growth to the corn and green grass to the meadows. The speaker himself had gone to the sacred mountains to pray at one time. But when he got there, no prayer came. He simply admired the scenery.

The southwestern Indians had kept their basically rich religion, the speaker went on, while tacking on a veneer of Catholic ceremonial to placate their Spanish conquerors. "But, of course," he stated flatly, "Christianity paled before the beautiful native religion that preceded the amalgam."

Orion became more alert. He had heard this charge over and over again from the young Indians of the Plains but even more from young Whites who tried to make amends for Custer's sins by asking their fellow palefaces to beat their breasts. These young people obviously demeaned the reality, personality, and teaching of Jesus Christ and idealized the ancient tribal beliefs. They ignored the intertribal wars, the torturing of the captives, the obscene rites in some of the villages.

The speaker concluded: "I have never met an Indian who was a real Christian." His tone suggested that in rejecting Jesus Christ the natives had chosen a nobler way to God. Orion bristled. He thought first of his grandmother, Emily Rising Moon, who, after the death of his mother, had taught him his religion and was to him the perfect embodiment of what a Christian should be. He called to mind his Arapahoe friend Golden Hawk, who had gone to Rome for the beatification of the Mohawk saint Kateri Tekawitha and met Pope John Paul II himself. He recalled the story of the Iroquois braves who traveled two thousand miles to bring a Blackrobe to the Salish of Montana back in the 1830s. His own Potawatomi ancestors had built the first Catholic church in the area of Chicago.

He remembered the words of a white friend, John Scott, who had gone to the Shrine of Our Lady of Guadalupe in Mexico: "After I looked long at the image of the Virgin," Scott had written, "I turned to glance at the Mexican Indians praying on their knees. The impact of those hundreds of faces, looking up at the image of Mary and completely absorbed in prayer, overwhelmed me! Each face was so alive with faith and devotion, so exalted by contact with the Divine! If ever I need to define a living faith, that would be it, so complete, so deep, so dynamic. It swept me along like a high tide and left me breathless with wonder and admiration."

Were these Mexican Indians not real Christians? He tried to keep quiet, to let the speaker's remark go unnoticed. But the temper he had inherited from his Irish grandfather overcame his native reserve. He rose to his full six feet two, pushed his unruly black hair back from his bronzed forehead, and in his rich voice blurted out: "You said you had never met an Indian who was a real Christian. That's a broad statement!"

The speaker looked defiantly at him. "Name one," he said.

The air was electric as Orion shot back: "I'll name one for a start—my grandmother, Emily Rising Moon."

Interest took the place of defiance in the face of the speaker. "I'd like to meet her," he said.

"Yes, you will," Orion responded. "If not in person, at least in my memories of her. . . ."

Here is Emily Rising Moon's story as Orion put it down. He preferred to tell it in the third person:

B

Emily Rising Moon

Orion Ruhane always felt that he owed his strong religious beliefs to his father's mother, his widowed grandmother, Emily Rising Moon. She was a woman of average height and sturdy frame, robust but not stout. Two braids of dark brown hair, the color of seasoned walnut, set off her round face. She wore a perpetually cherubic smile that reminded him of the angel who looked toward the Madonna on the main altar of their parish church in St. Mary's, Kansas. When Emily Rising Moon walked, erect and sure-footed, a grandchild usually clung to either hand. Her presence did not immediately stand out in a crowd, but those who looked at her a second time knew they were gazing at an unusual person.

Orion's father had an uncomplicated outlook on religion. "If you're Irish," Ryan Ruhane often said, "you're Catholic. And that's that!" Ryan went to Mass every day at the parish church. The Jesuit pastor had baptized him there in 1886. Ryan had married Renée Donnau at the church in 1928. In the course of time Ryan and Renée brought their three children for baptism. The father's faith was as much a part of the scenery as the broad cornfields in the bottomlands and the word of the Pope as sure as the ancient oak on the far terrace above the Kaw River.

When Orion's mother died in 1936, his grandmother stepped in to lift the gray November cloud that hung over the Ruhane home. Knowing that her son rarely talked of religious matters to his children, she took over the task. She deepened the faith of her grandchildren and their friends. In religion class at school, the children learned the answers to the catechism. They studied the commandments, the sacraments, the seven deadly sins, the many gifts of the Holy Spirit. And they got it all in their minds. But Emily Rising Moon touched their hearts.

Orion would never forget one of his grandmother's religious story sessions. He was then seven years old. His cousins had gathered at the Ruhane home for his father's birthday. After dinner the women worked in the kitchen. The men sat in the small room Orion's father used as a home office. They smoked their pipes and talked of Germany's growing strength under Hitler. The children gathered on the floor around

Grandmother's chair. The promised snow had held off, but the mid-December wind blew savagely across the open plains and made all of them even happier that the oak logs burned so warm in the fireplace.

"Keep your minds and hearts on Jesus," Grandma Rising Moon began. "Not on your pastor or the bishop or even the Holy Father in Rome. They all help, the Pope especially. He keeps his flock from wandering up dry gulches. And our missionary priest and bishop help. But if you put anything before Jesus—any person, any place, any thing—there's little the Pope, or the bishop or the missionary, or even your grandmother can do."

"No, Grandma," Orion's six-year-old cousin blurted out. "If any of us walked away from Jesus, and you told us to walk back, we would walk back."

"That may be so, little one," Grandmother responded gently. "But I won't always be around."

"Are you going somewhere, Grandma?" the little boy's sister broke in.

"Not yet, darling. But I hope someday to go where Jesus is. I don't know when that will be. He knows. Until you die, and go to his home, keep him first in your hearts." She paused. The youngsters sat in silence.

"Jesus Christ died on a cross for all of us," she went on. "He was the Son of God. He lived in Judea long ago; that's a land far across the great waters. When he reached the age of thirty, he went out from his little town and preached to the people. He gathered around him a group of fishermen and told them to be fishers of men. People asked him, 'Are you the Messiah, the one who the prophets told us would come?' He didn't say, 'Yes, I am.' Instead, he asked, 'What does Isaiah, the prophet, say about the Messiah?' He paused, gave them time to recall, then went on: 'The blind see, the lepers are cleansed, the poor have the good message preached to them!' That was exactly what Jesus was doing.

"Jesus went about doing good and taught that we should do only good things. We should love everybody. Not just our own tribe. Not just white men like your grandfather, but the Osage, the Cheyenne, the far-off Comanche, and the Mexicans who live even farther away."

She looked at one and then another, her eyes gathering them all in an embrace of affection. "Love all people as Jesus did. Your brothers and sisters. Your fathers and mothers, aunts, uncles, cousins, neighbors, everybody, even the boys and girls who may not treat you nice. That's what Jesus told us. Remember, too, that Jesus was close to the things about Him. He spoke of the birds of the air, the lilies of the field, the fig tree, the fish in the Lake of Galilee, the storm on the waters, the nets, the vines on the hillside, the sheep in the meadow, the grain ripe for harvest. Love all things God made, as Jesus did.

"St. Francis loved Jesus deeply. He called the sun 'Brother Sun' and the moon 'Sister Moon.' He saw God's hand in each and every one of the things God made. So you should try to see God's care for us in the rich kernels of corn that we will eat. See His glory in the colors of the sunset, His power in the storm. In Him we move and have our being."

And then in her marvelous voice, she sang "Everlasting Arms" and urged the children to sing with her. She stopped and smiled, and all smiled with her.

That lesson typified countless others. It was the same "Jesus-in-the-middle message," as the children called it, always in plain, direct language. She might speak of Jesus in the course of a talk on the tribal traditions, or while she spoke of football, a sport she enjoyed. She had seen a few games and listened to many on the radio. But Jesus was more alive to her than Jim Thorpe, whom she saw play and whose mother she knew, more real than the cottonwood in front of the house, more present than the dry wind that always blew across the rolling plains.

Grandma Rising Moon knew that knowing wasn't doing. One had to know what was right and have reasons to act on what was right. "The key to doing right," she told them as they grew older, "is this: Don't ask for trouble. Avoid it. Stay away from evil companions and dangerous places. And pray."

If any of the grandchildren might be tempted to do wrong, they would remember that she said, "Jesus is there looking at you."

Orion knew that his grandmother heard the voice of the Heavenly Father in the rush of the wind, in the burbling of the water in the stream, in the ecstatic song of the mockingbird, in the honking of the geese on their fall migration to the warm lands of the South. In Him she seemed to live, to move, to have her being; she saw His loveliness in the flowers of the spring, His glory in the autumn sunset, His strength in the tough hickory on the hillside, His gentleness in the lambs in the meadow. He was everywhere, with her all her days, as He had promised.

Little wonder that Orion Ruhane grew up with a strong faith! Orion believed that this centering of his life on Jesus, as his grandmother had taught him, gave him steadiness during the days of uncertainty. When the going got tough, he'd think of his grandmother and walk straight ahead. She taught him a second loyalty—loyalty to their tribe, the Neshnabek, the True People. Emily Rising Moon was a great storyteller in the tradition of her people.

II

The Story of the "True People"

A

THE NESHNABEK (1600)

The first time Emily Rising Moon told her grandchildren about the early days of the "True People" was back in 1939 when Orion was nine years old. The Ruhanes decided to take their grandmother with the family on a trip to the settlements where the Potawatomi had lived before they moved to Kansas. "War is coming in Europe," Ryan Ruhane had said. "Who knows whether we will be able to travel much if our country gets involved. Let's go now."

The Ruhanes drove to Kansas City and then north to Council Bluffs in Iowa where members of the tribe had lived before they moved to Kansas.

They drove across the cornfields of Iowa—through Des Moines to Iowa City then north to Cedar Rapids. From there they diagonaled to the Mississippi at Dubuque.

They turned north along the river toward the town of Marquette, Iowa. Their father took them to the top of a bluff where they could look east and see the spot where Louis Joliet and Father Marquette had come down the tamarack-colored Wisconsin and reached the Mississippi almost two hundred years before. They crossed the toll bridge into the old French town of Prairie du Chien, Wisconsin.

Ryan Ruhane had another reason for choosing this route. He wanted to stop at Campion Jesuit High School to visit a college classmate who was then a Jesuit teacher of English at the school. It was a happy reunion.

They drove east about sixty miles along the Wisconsin River, reversing the route of Father Marquette. When they arrived at the point where he and his companions had reached the river by portage, Ryan Ruhane turned the car northeast toward Green Bay. Orion had never imagined so many lakes and trees.

"Now I know, Grandmother," he said, "why you always said that great-grandmother's heart sank when she saw the treeless plains of Kansas."

When they reached a town called Wausaukee in the northeast corner of the state beyond Green Bay, they turned west to visit the Potawatomi Indian reservation. Emily Rising Moon spoke to her people in Neshnabek and brought from them a marvelous response. In the evening the Ruhanes gathered around a fire on the shore of Birch Lake. They sat on rough benches with newfound friends and cousins they had never met before.

"Tell us the story of the days when all our people lived up here along the bays and lakes, Grandma," Orion asked.

"It's a long story and a beautiful one, my children," Emily Rising Moon began. "A story I like to tell. One day the Master of All Life met some poor human beings in the land north of here on the far side of the greatest of the Lakes of Sweetwater. They told him they were the Neshnabek, the True People. 'And who are you?' they asked in turn.

"'I am the Master of All Life,' he replied. 'I will create anything you need. I will teach you how to lead a good, decent life.'

"That proved to be. The Master of All Life taught the True People how to make canoes from the birch trees you see all around you on the lake—trees of a kind we do not have on the Kansas prairie."

The youngsters from Kansas looked carefully at the many birch trees, the white bark resplendent in the light of a full moon that reflected across the waters. Orion had noticed these trees the first time that afternoon and had wondered what they might be.

"You see, grandchildren, we learn a lot by keeping our eyes open as we travel," Grandmother resumed. "But to go on with our story: The Master of All Life taught our ancestors to make bows and arrows, to mold pots, to weave baskets out of rushes from the marsh along the lake, and to build bark-covered wigwams. He showed them which animals and plants were good to eat and how to prepare them. He taught them how to plant and harvest corn, beans, and squash. He told them to keep peace among themselves, never to shed the blood of another Neshnabek; he told them to share and be equal." Grandmother smiled in joy. "Our people had been nothing before they found the Master of All Life. But now they were *something*: the beginning of a great people.

"In due time our ancestors moved south of the largest of the Lakes of Sweetwater and chose sites along the eastern shore of the Lake of the Illinois. They set up a dozen villages. They picked nuts and berries, hunted, and fished. Gradually, as generations went by, they began to till the soil. Crops were plentiful. Our ancestors increased in number and settled down in one area.

"The Neshnabek lived in peace with their neighbors and enjoyed the riches of the vast land. But word came that the Five Nations of the Iroquois had taken up the war club. They lived far away to the east, south of the easternmost of the large lakes. They set out to eliminate the Huron nation that lived between them and the Neshnabek. They killed many Huron braves, captured their women and children, and burned their villages."

"Five nations against one," a young cousin broke in. "That wasn't fair, Grandma!"

"That's right, little one, they did not heed the Master of All Life. Many Hurons fled the Iroquois to the villages of the Ojibway and Ottawa, cousins of the True People. The Iroquois followed them, relentless as winter wolves.

"Our ancestors wisely chose to flee trouble. They moved around the southern tip of the Lake of the Illinois, away from the wide range of the Five Nations. They turned north, and many of them set up villages near where we are now—on the western shore of the Lake of the Illinois, in the land of the Winnebago and Menominee. To their dismay, the Iroquois came on. With their swift canoes, hundreds of warriors raced down the western shore of the Lake of the Illinois. Tribesmen of smaller villages to the northeast saw them coming and sent a warning.

"The Neshnabek called a council. Should they flee further, beyond the reaches of the warrior canoes? That seemed to be the consensus of the elders in the early moments of the meeting. Then a young brave, Nimumiki, the Rising Moon, your ancestor, stood up. Back in their old homes to the east, the elders would not have listened to him. In fact, they would not have let him speak, had he hoped to do so. But not now!

"Rising Moon had been an ungainly youth. One of the old men said that his arms and legs grew too fast for the rest of him. And so it was. He had huge hands and feet, long and powerful arms, and short, thick legs below an undersized torso. Slowly and before anyone had noted it, his chest had filled out. He was strong but slow. And he was clever.

"When his fellow villagers fled as the Iroquois came, he was among those left to fend off the attackers as a rear guard. When most of the village had reached a place of temporary safety, the last of the defenders pulled back. Rising Moon, the slow one, soon fell far behind his fellows. The enemy made him their target and raced after him. He held his distance for a while, cleverly leading the Iroquois along a path away from the one the villagers had taken. The Iroquois tried a trick. While most of them held a steady pace, one warrior raced ahead of the pack to force Rising Moon to tire. Rising Moon ran faster. The young brave matched him stride for stride. Gradually, Rising Moon began to slow. But the man behind him failed to close the gap. Rising Moon knew it was a trick.

"The first racer fell back, and a second man came up from the larger body of the enemy. He came fast at first but gradually slowed down and held that pace. He did not try to come closer. The western sun had dropped behind a pine forest, and dusk was approaching. Rising Moon knew that the next warrior would try to capture or kill him."

"All the Iroquois against Rising Moon?" Orion's cousin broke in again. "That wasn't fair, Grandma!"

"That's right, little one. But our ancestor matched them all." Grandmother smiled and went on. "Rising Moon headed for a defile where large rocks might give him a chance to surprise his enemy. The wide-shouldered Iroquois raced into the uneven terrain with a long graceful stride intent only on closing in on Rising Moon and splitting his skull. But it was the Iroquois skull that split, as Rising Moon, from behind a huge granite boulder, sprang like a mountain cat behind the Iroquois and swung his tomahawk.

"Rising Moon wasted no time trying to hide the body and left it sprawled in the middle of the path. From the security of a distant wood, he looked back and saw his enemies pause as they reached their fallen comrade. Immediately alert, they scoured the area to see if the Neshnabek still hid nearby. They did not find him. Dusk was coming. The Iroquois decided to make camp.

"Rising Moon counted the Iroquois as they gathered sticks to make a fire. When he knew that all of them had settled down for the night, he moved steadily through the country he had come to know. Hungry, he found a few plums and blackberries and pushed on toward the security of a hidden cave. There he rested until dawn. All the next day, he led his pursuers away from our people. The Iroquois did not catch him. On the third morning, they gave up the hunt.

"Rising Moon diagonaled across the country to a place where he expected to meet his fellow Neshnabek. He ran with caution but without the tensions of the previous days. Weak from hunger and exertion, he reached our amazed people that evening. No one had expected to see him again. They realized that he had saved them by leading the Iroquois off the trail. But only slowly did they learn from him that he had ended the life of one of the enemy warriors."

Grandmother paused. None of the awed youngsters said a word. She took up her story. "When Rising Moon rose to speak at the council of the True People some months later, warriors, young and old, listened. 'We have gone far,' he began. 'Should we flee farther?' He paused, looked without fear at the circle around him, and went on: 'Should we instead stand up and defy them, conquer them or die like real Neshnabek? They have fierce warriors and stout war clubs. But their greatest weapon is the *fear* they put into the hearts of other people. Will that fear destroy us? I say, 'NO.'

"Murmurs of uncertainty from around the circle gave way to clenched fists and words of defiance. The voice of Rising Moon rang out, triumphant. 'I say we fight. We have five hundred warriors. The Menominee and the Winnebago can bring five hundred more. We can send runners to the villages of the Ottawa to let them know we are building a palisade near the shore to defend our people.'

"The palisade would have been nothing had the hearts of the defenders not been strong. But Rising Moon had made them iron. The Iroquois came, haphazardly at first. Those from the first canoes did not wait for the others to reach the shore. They attacked the wall immediately. The defenders held firm and sent a cloud of arrows at the enemy. The initial attackers fell back, pulling their wounded to the security of a pine grove.

"The Iroquois waited for more warriors and charged a second time. Once again the defenders drove the Iroquois back. Now the attackers knew they had an enemy who did not hear the word 'Iroquois' and lose heart. By this time all the warriors had reached the shore and had gathered around a war chief. The next attack would not be haphazard, as the first two were. The majority of the attackers still stood beyond the northeast corner of the fort around a war chief who seemed to be in charge, but Rising Moon noticed that two groups had slipped away quietly from the main body. These took positions in a cluster of willows to the northwest of the palisade, its weakest point. He guessed that the main blow would come there—after a noisy charge on the other corner.

"With a war cry that would have shaken a mountain lion, the Iroquois war chief sent his men directly toward the closest section of the wall. Again the steady stream of arrows from the defenders cut many down. But Rising Moon knew that this attack was only a trick.

"He ran to the northwest corner. The Winnebago braves crouched on a platform, invisible to the enemy. Rising Moon joined them on the platform. The Iroquois came in a wedge, a mighty chief leading it. Through a slit in the log palisade, Rising Moon watched the thickset enemy as he rushed forward brandishing a vicious war club in his left hand.

"Rising Moon slipped his thin, flint knife from its sheath, held it ready in his left hand, and gripped the war club in his right. The Iroquois reached the wall, grabbed the top of a log with his right hand, and tried to vault over the barricade. But Rising Moon pinned the hand of the chief to the top of the log and swung his war club on the skull of his foe. Blood drenched the Iroquois' chest. He hung for a moment. Then the weight of his body tore the flesh of his hand, and he fell to the ground, dead. The Winnebago warriors rose from their crouched positions and sent their arrows on the surprised hostiles like hail on an open field. The surviving Iroquois fell back.

"The attackers pulled their wounded out of the range of arrows from the fort and slunk back to the woods along the shore. As the sun went down in the west, an endless string of Iroquois canoes moved back up the lake. It was obvious; defeat was something the Iroquois rarely faced. They never returned to the area of the western lakes to kill other tribesmen.

"Over the years the storytellers recounted the exploits of Rising Moon. Later generations began to call him the Slayer of Iroquois, and he became a legendary figure. We, his descendants, share his prestige."

The children sat in silence. Even the little boy who was so upset that the Five Nations had destroyed one tribe had nothing to say. A whippoorwill began its monotonous dirge.

"Tomorrow night, more legends," Grandmother said with a smile. "That was enough for one night. Perhaps too much. Tomorrow I will tell you of the coming of the white man."

B

THE COMING OF THE FRENCH (1650)

T he next day Orion spent meeting relatives he had only heard about and making new friends. "Your grandmother—she's a wonderful storyteller" was the usual greeting. "We shall hear her again tonight." The day went fast.

Weather reports told of sultry temperatures on the Plains. But Wisconsin wore its friendliest face, brisk and cool. Orion had been surprised when his father had told him to take his coat on the trip. Who needs a jacket in July? Orion had thought. Now he was happy that he had listened to his father.

When Orion and his family brought their grandmother to the village center for the evening festivities, far more people had already come than were present the night before. Elders sat around a drum, beating a steady tattoo. Occasionally, a baritone chanted a line of a song. Orion did not understand the words. His grandmother explained their meaning and the origin of the chant. The drum beat on. No one seemed in a hurry.

The night before, the campfire and the storyteller seemed to come together by chance. But now ritual prevailed. At no apparent signal the drums stopped. The Chief of the village arose. "A daughter of our greatest hero, Rising Moon," he began, "has come among us. When she arrived, the summer heat left our village, the birds began to sing, the fish found their way into our nets, and the chipmunks winked at each other in glee. Our guest is one of the matchless storytellers of our people. She will tell many things our children have never heard and our old people may have forgotten."

A young man brought a comfortable folding chair from his car for Emily Rising Moon. She thanked him and then thanked the Chief for his kind words.

"My brothers and sisters of the Wisconsin Neshnabek," she began, her voice as clear as a mission bell, her words resounding over the crackle of burning logs. "I am happy to speak to you. I am even happier to tell stories to the children. Last night we heard how our braves drove back the warriors of the Five Nations and brought peace to the area. Shortly before that, young men of our people went in their canoes far to the east, to the land of the Hurons who were our friends. These young men came back with stories of curious creatures who looked like human beings but wore strange clothes, had light eyes, and wore an ugly matting of hair on their faces.

"Their medicine was strong, their tools magical. They had thin, slick, shining knives that cut easily. Their sleek, sharp tomahawks could have cleaved the stoutest shagbark. They carried smoke-sticks that spat arrows one could not see and killed everything that stood in their way.

"The Hurons said that these strange ones came from across the wide water. One day, shortly after the Iroquois went away, one of these light faces from a place called France came west with a Huron guide. From his canoe, he saw a group of the True People making a fire. He asked his Huron guide: 'Who are these people?'

"The Huron thought he had asked: 'What are they doing?' and answered, 'They are making a fire!'

"What the Frenchman heard sounded like 'Potawatomi.' That's what he remembered. It meant puffing out one's cheeks to start a fire. So to the white man the True People became the People of the Fire, the Potawatomi.

"When the first Frenchman came, our people looked upon him as a spirit chief who used iron tools and weapons. They were surprised that he was shaped like a human being, much like them except for his beard. He was less strong than many of them. He needed food. He got sick. If cut, he bled. He said he needed a woman to take care of his wigwam. He had tools and trinkets that the tribe wanted. He traded them for furs and skins the hunters gathered. In the spring he left for the places of the French. But in the fall he came back with others like him.

"The elders agreed to welcome the matted-face ones. Gradually, trade between new arrivals and the Neshnabek grew. It proved a boon to both. Our people dealt with the smaller tribes of the area and so became the middlemen between the white-eyes and them. With the French as our allies, we became the favored nation among all those of the western lakes.

"No women came with these traders. As a result, more and more of them took wives of our people. The elders of the tribe had different views about this. Some thought it a good thing, since it would seal the friendship. Others wondered if the French could fit in with the tribal ways. Were these men perhaps wanderers by nature? Would they stay a while and then leave or go on a trading journey back to the Rock of Quebec and never return? And what if children came? Membership in the clan went through the male line. These children would be lost in the middle. Many young men were not happy. Their sisters were looking to the matted-faced ones and ignoring them. Would peace remain in the villages? Our people could only wait and see.

"The Great Medicine Man of the French came about that time. The Neshnabek had heard about him from their neighbors to the east and from their own young men who had gone to the Rock of Quebec with trading expeditions. His name was Claude Allouez. He wore a black robe and he talked about the Master of Life. He had come west some years before with a band of Ottawa traders. On the way, one of the Ottawa chiefs became convinced that the Blackrobe would pour water over the heads of the Ottawa children and hurt them. He wanted none of the Blackrobe's magic. He left the Frenchman alone on a rocky island. But another Ottawa felt that his fellow had betrayed the hospitality of the tribe. He feared what the Chief of the French back in Quebec would do in return for their failure to keep their word. He brought the Blackrobe to the western village. But the view of the other chief eventually prevailed. The Ottawa disdained the message of the Blackrobe.

"The Neshnabek opened their ears. The older men, the women, and the children listened when the Blackrobe told them what the Master of Life had done, how he sent his son Jesus as Savior to teach all people how to live as the Master of Life wanted. He told them that they were all children of the Master of Life, that he loved all his children on earth, and that he wanted them to love each other.

"Few young men listened until Rising Moon did. Then many others followed. They liked the fact that the Blackrobe demanded better conduct of the few French traders who lived among them. He wanted them to stand before him with their Neshnabek wives and promise fidelity. He told them that they themselves should not drink the fatal *eau de vie* or give it to the men of the village.

"When the Neshnabek began to understand what the Blackrobe was saying, they saw that he was not denying their ancestral beliefs but explaining them and adding to them. They had believed in good and bad spirits. He did, too, and told the people how to take the good and hold back the bad. He told them to love their neighbors. This they had always done. No Neshnabek lacked anything if others could help him. The Blackrobe wanted them to love their enemies. That was no problem. They had no enemies except the Iroquois, who lived far away and by that time had left them alone. Eventually, the Neshnabek came to accept the teaching of the Blackrobe that Jesus was the Savior of all and the Master of Life was father of all people.

"An even more famous Blackrobe—his statue is in Washington among the heroes—came to a village of our ancestors near where we are now. His name was Jacques Marquette. He had just returned from going down the Great River almost to its mouth with six other Frenchmen. No one had done it before and returned to tell about it.

Most of the French were short and square built with dark hair. He walked erect, looking over the heads of his companions. When he took off his wide-brimmed black hat, his hair shone in the sun, the color of corn. He was born, like all the French, in their land beyond the seas. He had come to us from the distant city of the French by the Rock of Quebec. He had braved the threats of the Iroquois. He had carried his share of the burden at the Ottawa portage. He had come for many miles to see us, to bring our ancestors the good news that Jesus brought to earth.

Later he traveled on his last journey along the

wintry shore of the Lake of the Illinois. Some of our ancestors were with him. Two of them and three Frenchmen stood by as he uttered the names of Jesus and Mary. He kissed the cross that one of the men held to his lips. And then he died, a man who had not yet seen the cycle of the years for the fortieth time. We will never forget him; we never could. He had canoed the length of the Great River—and come back. And he had one task in life, to tell all people of the love of the Great Spirit. Three hundred years have gone by, and we still remember his name."

Grandmother Rising Moon paused, looked at us, and said, "All of you Ruhanes, remember. We saw the place where Father Marquette and his friends reached the Great River."

"That was a beautiful place, Grandma," Orion's little sister said.

Emily Rising Moon looked from one child to another. The birch logs had burned down. The moon had fallen behind a thick stand of evergreens. The children were getting sleepy. The whippoorwill sang his repetitive dirge.

"It is getting late," Grandmother said. "There will be other times for other stories. Let us all say our night prayer we learned at school. All together: Angel of God, my guardian dear," she began, and all joined in, "to whom his love commits me here. Ever this day be at my side, to light, to guard, to rule, to guide."

Orion was surprised that his Wisconsin cousins knew the prayer. He had always thought it was the special prayer of his own school.

C

THE POWERFUL POTAWATOMI (1765–1830)

On one occasion when he was still in elementary school, Orion had gone with his father to an intertribal gathering at Haskell Institute at Lawrence, Kansas, a school attended by young people of various tribes. He heard a leader of the Potawatomi say that the True People had been the strongest nation in the area of the Great Lakes.

An Ottawa countered, "No! Our people under Pontiac!"

A Miami elder held for the Shawnee. Orion decided to ask his grandmother. He picked an interesting time. The January days had been cold but not cold enough to freeze the ponds for skating. Too little snow had fallen for sledding. A raw wind drove Orion home from school "on the double." He came in, greeted his grandmother, took off his heavy jacket, and relaxed in the warmth of the kitchen. His grandmother was baking apple pies. She placed the last pie in the oven and sat down at the kitchen table.

"Grandmother, I heard you tell of the early days and of the coming of the French. Were our people the most powerful nation in those days?"

"My grandson," Emily Rising Moon answered, "it is not really important which tribe was most powerful. The Ottawa were mighty when Pontiac led them. Many of our young men took part in his battles. The Shawnee under Tecumseh were unbeatable. Your great-grandfather met many of them when they first moved to Kansas. But our ancestors were courageous, too, our warriors many. Our villages controlled the waterways between the French in Canada and those living in the Mississippi Valley, which included the Wisconsin, the Illinois, and the Wabash Rivers. Our allies, the French, built Fort Duquesne where the Allegheny and the Monongahela Rivers come together. They controlled the Ohio Valley."

Emily Rising Moon paused. She rose from her chair. "Let me get an atlas so I can point out these places on a map as we go along."

"Keep your seat, Grandmother," Orion said and walked into the front room. He took the atlas from the top of the bookshelf and handed it to his grandmother.

She opened the map book to the area below Lake Erie. Pointing to Pittsburgh, she said, "The

French built Fort Duquesne here at the junction of the Allegheny and the Monongahela Rivers. In the spring of 1755 our people and other tribes sent their young men to help the French defend the fort. The British sent a big force under a general by the name of Braddock. He was famous only because he lost that battle. History books call it 'Braddock's Defeat,' not a French victory. George Washington led the troops from the English colonies on the Atlantic coast. He knew how to fight in the rough country. Braddock was used to open battlefields where the soldiers could see their enemy." Emily Rising Moon smiled. "I'm sure you have heard of George Washington. What about General Braddock?"

"We have American History every year from the fifth grade on, Grandma. We heard all about Braddock."

"You're becoming observant, my grandson," Emily Rising Moon said. "I knew you knew of Washington, our first president. I'm happy that you also heard of General Braddock. He gave the Neshnabek a chance for our greatest victory.

"When our young men arrived at Fort Duquesne, they did not want to fight behind a wall. Let the French man the wall. Our braves would prevent the British from wheeling their cannon against the fort. The British were marching on a trail that would lead them through a narrow defile not too far away. The chiefs of all tribes sent their young men into thickets on both sides of this rocky draw. They gave one order: 'Hold your fire until the entire red line moves into the ravine.'

"This order was not easy for the excited young men. Many of them had never seen a British soldier before. Some had never faced cannon fire. The fearful music of the Scottish bagpipes made many want to flee. But they held their places in the thickets. The proud Redcoats marched into the trap. With flags flying, bands playing, arms swinging in cadence, the Black Watch, a Scottish regiment whose men wore skirts into battle, led the British to their doom."

Orion wanted to ask about men who would go into battle wearing skirts. But his Grandmother's account had so gripped him that he put that thought out of his mind.

His grandmother continued her story: "Suddenly a shot rang out. Then another. Then flame and smoke. Horses reared in panic and men screamed in horror. Death came at the enemy from tangled thickets. It was as if leaves became bullets and arrows. General Braddock fell, his horse shot from under him. He leaped on another mount that had lost its rider. He urged his men into a battle line as if he were on a parade ground. At last he went down, badly wounded."

Orion almost felt as if he had been in that battle, so vivid was his Grandmother's picture.

"Only Colonel George Washington of the Virginia militia was to salvage anything on that dismal day for the British," Grandmother went on. "He held his place at the end of the line and put order in the retreat. Of course it was not a dismal day for our ancestors. They gathered their share of the booty. They rounded up many British horses to carry their spoils. These animals formed the basis of the herd that pulled our wagons on the journey to Kansas years later. Our warriors joined with those of other western tribes to win another great victory over the British at Fort Ticonderoga on Lake Champlain. But in the end, without the Neshnabek and other warriors, the French General Montcalm lost to the British General Wolfe on what they call the Plains of Abraham near Quebec City. The French surrendered and pulled all their troops out of the North American continent."

Emily Rising Moon paused. Good teacher that she was, she made Orion repeat the main thread of what she had recounted. She listened with satisfaction as he recalled the story in great part. "You have the makings of a historian," she said.

Emily Rising Moon rose, walked to the oven and checked the pies. Orion could not resist looking over her shoulder. The pies were turning a rich brown. "I'll give them a few more minutes," she said. Then she went on with her account: "Our ancestors had lost no battles. But our allies, the French, left the country. We were no longer the favored nation. The British had different ways and attitudes we did not like.

"In a few years the British were at war again, this time with their own colonists. As you can recall from your grade school history, George Washington led the army of the English colonies. He was the man our braves faced at Fort Duquesne. The Neshnabek were now uncertain. Should we fight with the British, who seemed to want us, or with the colonists? Some of our young men fought on both sides in different places during the struggle. The French army and navy came to the rescue of Americans and helped them win.

"When the war ended, white men poured over the rugged mountains into the valley of the Ohio River. They came like the Chosen People in the Old Testament intent on driving the Canaanites out of the Promised Land. We were the Canaanites in their minds, and we had the promised lands.

"Our young men won two battles to hold the white men back but lost at a place called Fallen Timbers in 1795." Emily Rising Moon pointed to the atlas again. "Fallen Timbers is here, where Toledo, Ohio, is today."

Emily Rising Moon turned the pages of the atlas to the map of the War of 1812. "By the time of the colonists' second war with Great Britain," she said, "our homelands still extended from the western tip of Lake Erie to the Mississippi River. The Whites lived along the Ohio River far to the south. Our villages spread through fifty miles on either side of what the Whites called the boundary of the State of Ohio and the Territory of Indiana. To the north, our people lived along the western shore of the Lake of the Illinois—the Whites called it Lake Michigan—as far as Green Bay. By this time our ancestors, like the white settlers on the frontier, farmed a few acres and hunted and fished. Many Neshnabek joined the Shawnee Chief Tecumseh fighting on the side of the British against the colonists, only to lose decisively along the Thames River in Canada.

"From then on, through the next decades, we made treaty after treaty with the Whites, selling our land bit by bit. With the decline of the fur trade, our people had to depend on the white man's goods. We would sell a bit of our land to get enough money to carry on. One treaty followed another. Then President Andrew Jackson decided to move all people to the Great Plains. The Whites thought it was a desert that they would never want. Most of our people decided to move. But not those in Michigan. Leopold Pekogan led them. My grandmother knew him well. A strong, smart man. He saved his land for his people. Others moved to northern Wisconsin.

"That's today's history lesson." Grandmother smiled. "Now we'll see how well you listened."

Orion began slowly, relying on the atlas. He always studied maps carefully. His grandmother listened attentively. "A good *B* grade," she said. "You do well for a born dreamer." She knew he was fighting Braddock while she talked of other events.

By that time, the aroma of baking applies told them that the pies would soon be ready. "A *B* grade deserves one piece of pie," she said, as she took the pies from the oven.

Orion took one bite of the steaming pie. "This pie deserves an A-plus, Grandma."

D

KANSAS-BOUND
(1830–1860)

Every year on Memorial Day Orion's father took his mother and his three children in the Studebaker to the parish cemetery. It dominated the hill to the north of the town. His father left them and promised to pick them up an hour later. Memorial Day was not a holiday that year at the co-op where he worked.

Orion noticed the graves with new flags on them. The attack on Pearl Harbor the previous December had made the townspeople more aware of the men who had fought in previous wars. Many newly placed flowers sent a fragrance into the air. A light dew remained on the grass. Grandmother led the Ruhanes to the oldest part of the cemetery. She stopped at the grave of her own grandmother and led the children in prayer. Then she told them what her own grandmother had often told her.

"Pere Jean St. Cyr had baptized her. The Chief of the Blackrobes in St. Louis, Bishop Joseph Rosati, sent him. Our ancestors, with the help of some French traders, built the first church there. The area later gained the name Chicago, after one of our chiefs, Shi-shak. Our ancestors worshipped in that church only a short time.

"A few years later, Chief Blackhawk and his Sauk warriors came back across the Mississippi homesick for their ancestral lands along the Rock River in northern Illinois. The white settlers who had taken their lands tried to stop them but failed. Regular troops came in and drove the Sauk back to Iowa Territory. Our ancestors did not join Blackhawk's braves. But some Whites did not know one tribe from another and killed several of our unarmed people. Many of our braves would have reacted in fury, but our wise chiefs held the young men in check. Our ancestors kept the peace, and what was their reward? Orders to move.

"The True People had lived in woods alive with deer and elk and smaller animals whose fur kept them warm in long winters. They lived along rivers and lakes filled with fish. They traveled by canoes over endless waters and lived in houses made of bark and willow. Now they were to move to the dry rolling plains without trees, where the endless barren lands stretched from the rising of the sun to its setting.

"Our family had been living then in the area around the Twin Lakes near the northern boundary of the State of Indiana. In September 1838, soldiers rounded up over eight hundred of our people and forced them to march at gunpoint along the Wabash and then west.

"How could otherwise good Christian people do something like this to fellow Christians? Some explained the crime by saying that the Whites who pushed our people from our lands were Old Testament readers who looked upon themselves as God's chosen ones and on the Neshnabek as the Canaanites, to be driven out."

Grandmother was puzzled. Gloom flooded her face as she went on. "That could be. I once read a letter from a doctor in Philadelphia to a botanist in England at the time of the French and Indian War. He predicted that 'true Oliverian predestinarians'—I suppose he meant the Puritan followers of Oliver Cromwell—'whom God had made on purpose to kill the French and Indians, would soon drive every dog of them out of North America, or out of the world.' The soldiers who drove our people from our homelands certainly looked upon us as hindrances to their advance, if not as dogs.

"One consoling fact of this time was the presence of Father Benjamin Petit, a young French missionary of the diocese of Vincennes. He had volunteered to work among us and identified with us. He practiced law in France before he undertook studies for the priesthood. He wanted to work with government agents to get a better arrangement for our people. But Bishop Simon Bruté allowed no such approach, as Leopold Pekogan in Michigan.

"Petit was a scholarly priest, not a rugged

outdoorsman. I often have contrasted him with Father Peter John DeSmet, the Jesuit among the Salish and other tribes of the mountain West who passed through Kansas on his early journeys to the mountains. But he hazarded the trail. Had Father Petit not, some of our young men might have wanted to fight. Their effort could have brought on a massacre.

"Our people were driven by state militia down the Wabash then across Illinois and northern Missouri to Kansas City and again south to Sugar Creek—a distance of 850 miles.

"During that same year, 1838, the Cherokee were driven from their homes in the Southeast. Their 'Trail of Tears' became part of American lore, our 'Trail of Death' was forgotten. But the journey of our ancestors was equally trying for the average person. All types of weather faced our people—heat in the late summer, rain in the fall, and winter cold in early December.

Food had been promised but often was not available. Many people had to walk. They wore out their moccasins or their shoes. There were no replacements. It was either walk on your bare feet over rough roads or crowd into wagons. Each day another child or an elder died.

"Whites along the line of march had varied reactions. Some were curious, others hostile. A few, especially in Catholic towns, were friendly. Father Petit offered Mass every day, to the amazement of Protestants, who thought we were barbarous warriors. Many died on the way, mostly infants and aged.

Finishing the journey, Father Petit grew seriously weak, with rashes, open sores, fever and headaches. Then word came that the bishop wanted him to return immediately to Indiana. He set out in winter with one companion. By the time he reached St. Louis, his cassock was torn, his illness was acute, and he stopped at the Jesuit university community. Two bishops visited him there—Bishop Joseph Rosati of St. Louis and Bishop Mathias Loras of Dubuque. They and Father John Elet, the Superior of the Jesuits, were with him when, shortly after midnight on the night of February 10, he passed away. A martyr of dedication! We can never forget him.

Father Christian Hoecken, a Belgian Blackrobe who had known some of our people at Council Bluffs in Iowa Territory, met them at Sugar Creek. He talked of the Master of All Life, as the French Blackrobes Jacques Marquette and Claude Allouez had done two hundred years before. He made our people feel welcome.

"Kansas wasn't Indiana or Michigan. But our ancestors came to like Sugar Creek. 'The Woman Who Always Prayed,' a French nun, Philippine Duchesne, had taught Osage and Iowa girls at her school near St. Louis. She always wanted to visit our villages. A chance came. Even though along in years, she made the trip by steamboat to Westport near Kansas City and then by wagon over rough roads to our villages. Our young men rode out on horseback to greet her. She stayed a year among us. During the rest of her life, her friends told us, she would tell what a joyful welcome our mounted braves gave her. Our ancestors never forgot her. They knew that the Master of All Life talked to her in a way he did not talk to the rest of us. Several families named their daughters after her."

Orion's grandmother led the family to a grave that had the name Philippine Rising Moon on its headstone. "My mother and your great-grandmother," she said and led the children in another prayer.

The day had begun cloudy, but now a warming sun broke through the May clouds. Orion took off his jacket.

"When your great-great-grandmother was twenty years old," Emily Rising Moon went on, "the White Father in Washington told our ancestors to move here. The new place straddled the Kaw River at a site four days' journey from where it flowed into the Big Muddy. It was not as nice as Sugar Creek. My grandmother often told me how sad she felt when she looked in every direction and saw no trees, no lakes, no growing things, only barren hillsides. She stood on a hill like this one and looked north, south, east, and west and saw nothing! It was as if one could peer over the rim of the world without hope."

Almost automatically Orion looked to the ridge beyond the Kaw. Then he turned and looked behind him. As his grandmother had said, it was as if he stood on a giant sphere and saw over its rim.

"The wind blew," Emily Rising Moon went on," just as it is blowing today. Endlessly, chapping the lips, drying the land, parching the corn. Endless wind and unbroken horizon. And coyotes howling all night. My grandmother never came to like it.

"She told of a new and surprise danger. The tribes of the High Plains—the Pawnee, the Cheyenne, and the Sioux—had not asked our people to come and did not want us. On their fast ponies they raided the villages of the newly arriving tribes—the Shawnee, the Miami, the Seneca, one of the Five Nations.

"Fortunately, our ancestors had captured horses from General Braddock in the French-English War. Many of our young men rode well. A band of Sioux attacked one of our villages. Our young men drove them off. The Sioux had not expected defenders on horseback. Other tribes from the East were not so lucky." Emily Rising Moon smiled. "You children may find this hard to accept. My grandmother told me something that no one believes when I tell them. The white chiefs put their soldiers on horseback to defend the woodland tribes from the raiders. Imagine, pony soldiers protecting Shawnee from the Pawnee!"

Grandmother smiled. "No one believes when I tell them. They can look it up in the history books. The Whites called the pony soldiers 'Dragoons.' We called them 'Dragons.'

"Our ancestors needed the Blackrobes more than they needed the pony soldiers," Emily Rising Moon said as she led the family over to the priests' plot. "The Jesuit missionaries came from Missouri and set up a school for our children. The Blackrobe my grandmother talked about most was Maurice Gailland." Emily Rising Moon pointed to his grave.

Orion read the words: "Maurice Gailland, S.J.,

born in Bagnes, Switzerland, October 27, 1815, ordained Lausanne, April 11, 1846, died St. Mary's, August 12, 1877."

Emily Rising Moon went on with her story. "Even though he grew up in the beautiful mountains of Switzerland, Father Gailland came to love the Kansas plains in a way my grandmother never did. He also said that our language, as the Greek's, flowed like honey. The only Greek words our ancestors ever heard were the words *Kyrie eleison, Christe eleison*, at Mass. Blackrobe Gailland had our people repeat the Kyrie in Greek and then in our language: "Jesos, ofchiban juwenita osichin, Jesos, oviya niscetin, Jesos, omiskim, minechin.' They both sounded beautiful. Father Gailland also wrote a dictionary of our language, a history of the True People, and a prayer book in Neshnabek. My mother had a copy. It was printed in Cincinnati in 1865, right after the White Man's War."

Emily Rising Moon turned and walked slowly to the gate of the cemetery. "Not all our people followed the words of the Blackrobe. Some kept intact all the old ways. They called themselves the 'Prairie Band.' When the missionaries opened schools for boys and girls, "the Catholics were happy. The Prairie Band ignored the Blackrobes. All the while the Oregon Trail brought countless Whites through our territory.

"During the White Man's War many Whites moved onto our lands. President Lincoln freed the Blacks but wanted to send us away. Our ancestors said, 'No!' After the war, President Johnson worked out a more acceptable agreement. Our people could move to Indian Territory, take tillable acres near St. Mary's, or settle on a smaller reservation north of the mission. My father, your great-grandfather, was like the first Rising Moon. No one could budge him. He took land, worked hard, and, with your grandfather Patrick's help, prospered."

The face of Emily Rising Moon had reflected her chagrin at the Government's failure to keep its promises. She brightened and went on: "Jesus made us feel at home in Kansas. We were not long at St. Mary's before He sent a message to us. A young boy was walking at the north edge of the bottomland near the mission school. A storm threatened from the southwest. The boy saw the funnel cloud sweep across the ridge in the far distance beyond the Kaw River.

"He prayed the Hail Mary. Jesus' mother told him that big winds would go away from St. Mary's. That storm passed by and so has every one since. Even though we are in the path of many cyclones, Mary takes care of us."

"Did you know that little boy who saw the Virgin Mary, Grandma?" Orion's brother asked.

"Yes, Grandson, my mother pointed him out to me as we entered church one Sunday. He was a thin, wiry boy, quiet and soft spoken. He had told his mother of the vision, and no one else. She told the priest."

"Do you believe he saw Jesus' Mother?" the boy asked.

"Many people saw the storm cloud coming. They saw it turn and move on down the ridge away from St. Mary's. My grandmother said it was something all noticed. And then they heard the message of Our Lady." Emily Rising Moon smiled. "My grandmother knew we had been blessed. But the little boy never talked about it, and our pastor told us never to bother him about it."

"And what did he do later, Grandma?"

"He lived right here in St. Mary's, worked a ranch, raised cattle, married in our church—just like the rest of us. His grandchildren still live south of town. She pointed toward the distant ridge beyond the Kaw. At that moment, Orion's father drove up to take them home.

Years later, Orion often thought how much more interesting his grandmother had been than even his best history teacher in school.

III

Family Backgrounds

A

Out of Ruma (1878)

"What brought Grandfather to Kansas?" Orion asked his grandmother an early June evening. The two sat on the wide veranda of the Ruhane home. It looked to the south. The day had been warm; but as the sun set, a gentle breeze drifting across a wide field of clover cooled and sweetened the air.

"Well, Grandson, I think you know how little your grandfather said about anything. He said even less about his family back in Illinois. I never pressed him to find out more about them. I did see his baptismal certificate from St. Patrick's Parish in Ruma, Illinois. The town was called O'Harasburg then. Your grandfather was born on June 21, 1858. His parents were William Ruhane and Ellen McDonough, natives of the town of Spiddal in County Galway, Ireland.

"His parents gave him the name of Patrick Sarsfield after an Irish hero. His mother died a few years later. That's all I ever heard from your grandfather. Most information I got from Patrick's cousin Billy Macauley. After Patrick's mother died, depression gripped his father. An older brother John took care of the Ruhane farm. He and Patrick often clashed. Their oldest sister, Mary, ran the household like a jail. Life was not pleasant for your grandfather.

"I never knew these in-laws. Your grandfather never seemed anxious that we get together, even on one occasion when we traveled to St. Louis. Ruma was not too far away from the city.

"Billy Macauley knew that Patrick wanted to get away from his brothers and sisters. Billy showed Patrick a notice he had found on the door of his parish church after Mass one Sunday in St. Louis. Billy returned regularly to visit his family in Ruma. A priest by the name of Thomas Ambrose Butler had put up the notice. He had earlier worked in Kansas and wanted to start an Irish colony not far from here near Blaine. You would not remember, but once it was called Butler City.

"Billy Macauley showed me the notice and told me the story. On a pleasant fall day when Billy came down to see your grandfather, the two of them sat under the thick foliage of a box elder tree in the front yard of the Ruhane home. Billy smoked his pipe, and Patrick munched on a Calhoun County apple. I remembered that fact because your grandfather always insisted that Kansas never had apples like those from Calhoun County, Illinois.

"'Look at this,' Cousin Billy said, showing him the message of Father Butler. It was one of those warm fall days that make you think October will last forever. A steady south wind brought the smell of burning leaves from a neighboring home. Billy would give you all possible details of every story. He was as talkative as your grandfather was silent. 'It's a plan of Father Butler,' Billy went on. 'He worked out west for a while and now he wants to start an Irish colony on the plains of Kansas.'

"'Makes sense, Billy,' Patrick said. He finished his apple and threw the core away.

"'Father TAB's got the whole thing figured out,' Billy went on. 'By the way, he always signs his letters TAB, so people call him Father TAB. A group of wealthy Irish businessmen will help the program get going down the rails. They set up a colonization board. Organized a stock company. Purchased twelve thousand acres from the Union Pacific Railroad.' Billy paused, read your grandfather's approval, and went on. 'The colonization board will make loans for tools and seeds for those like you and me who don't have any ready cash. The land costs $3.60 an acre, and we will have eleven years to pay. Even if we had two or three bad years, we would have eight or nine good years, and the land will be ours.'

"Billy proved right about that. He and your grandfather paid their loan in five years. Two good crops. Then a bad one. Then two good. But let's get back to Billy and your grandfather sitting under the box elder tree on the warm fall day.

"Billy next told Patrick that Father TAB wanted the young men who moved to Kansas to know that they would not have trouble meeting Catholic girls. The Potawatomi and Osage girls had learned their religion at Mission Schools. They made good wives and were as pretty as Irish girls."

"Grandpa must have agreed with Father TAB, Grandma," Orion said.

"I'm sure he did," his grandmother said with a smile. "But not Billy Macauley. He was a confirmed bachelor, but many of our girls liked him. Billy said that Father TAB had signed up forty men. He needed twenty more to make a success of the Kansas plan. Now, Grandson, you didn't know Billy. He could sell anything. Corn in Kansas. Tobacco in Kentucky. But this time he had something good to sell.

"When your grandfather agreed to go, Cousin Billy worked out the details. He knew that Patrick's brother and sister would never approve of their going. Sometimes I would sense from what Billy said that Patrick's sister spoke badly about the idea and belittled Billy for planning to leave. She never dreamed that Patrick would go along. Whatever she said made Patrick even more anxious to go.

"Throughout the succeeding weeks your grandfather stayed at his tasks on the farm and kept his mouth shut." Grandmother smiled. "Of course, that wasn't hard for him. Cousin Billy went back to Ruma for Christmas. The two men laid their final plans. Father Butler had chosen the first day of February 1878 for the final meeting of those who were going west in the spring. The group met at St. Patrick's Hall in St. Louis. Billy and Patrick met with the colonization board and their fellow Kansans-to-be on that night. The next morning they boarded the Missouri Pacific train for Kansas City and rode the Union Pacific to a flag stop where Butler City would soon be. And that's all I ever heard about it."

B

Father Butler's Boys

Orion's grandmother loved to tell the story of the coming of "Father Butler's Boys," as the people of Kansas—Indian and white—called them when they came out in that year, 1878. Orion remembered when the entire family gathered at the old farmhouse for Grandmother's seventieth birthday back in 1938. It was a beautiful day in early October. The willows and the cottonwoods down by the creek had already turned yellow, and the ashes and maples around the house were brilliant in early fall colors. The air was clear, the corn stood high in the bottomlands. The cattle grazed on the hillsides.

"At first, I did not like Patrick Ruhane," Emily Rising Moon began. "When I first saw him, I found him menacing. He had a hulking frame and was so tall that he had to lean over when he walked in a doorway. I guess that's why he always worked with his head and broad shoulders bent over. He and Cousin Billy sowed their corn and their wheat early. They built their sod house on a piece of land not far from where we lived."

Emily Rising Moon rocked in her chair. "I'll give *this* to Billy Macauley," she went on. "Not a hard worker like your grandfather but a shrewd man. He picked the land wisely. It had a creek running through it, good drainage, a fine level stretch of rich soil, and a section of woods. On that prairie, wood was gold. Cousin Billy handled his timber better than he did his fields. He knew the trees to cut and those to keep. He knew how to space them, as you can see out there." She pointed with her cane. "That forest is still intact even though we have been living off of it for this long time. Billy and your grandfather set their sod house against a southeast sloping hill. That way, they did not have to build up the walls all the way around. The hillside itself provided protection on the entire back and much of the two sides. The floor was dirt, but it was cool in summer, like all sod houses. And as long as there was fire, it was warm in winter.

"Since there were only girls in our family, and my father ran cattle, we needed help. When your grandfather finished his own chores he would come over and help my father. I was only ten when he came."

Grandmother paused and looked up as she heard the honking of the first wedge of geese that the Ruhanes had seen that fall. Her hearers all turned to watch the graceful flight. When the geese had passed out of sight, she resumed her tale. "My father and your grandfather worked well together from the beginning. Gradually, a friendship grew. But I was still scared of your grandfather. He was so serious, even glum. It was as if the Irish famine was about to strike Eastern Kansas. All he ever said was, 'Makes sense!' He said that even when what somebody said was stupid."

She paused as several other hearers who remembered Patrick couldn't suppress a chuckle.

"Cousin Billy, for his part, was always happy," she resumed. "Life was like a spring of bubbling water when he was around."

The children always liked to hear of Cousin Billy. None of them had ever met him. He was a myth, a wraith, a person who might not have existed in reality but only in family memories.

"After several years," Grandmother went on, "Cousin Billy left the farm to your grandfather and took a job at a store in Butler City. Oh how we missed him! But your grandfather slowly grew on us. We were all girls, and he became like the big brother that we didn't have." Grandmother smiled, and her eyes were even brighter than usual. "Your grandfather wanted to be my godfather when the bishop came out to confirm us. By that time your grandfather had built this frame house, hauling the lumber up from Wamego on the U-P tracks. It was not a beautiful home but was spacious, rambling, and comfortable. One day I realized that he no longer was an older brother to me but that I loved him. I came to realize it in this way. He had done something the day before that made me angry. I spoke critically of him. My little sister Rosalie was the only one who heard me.

"She blurted out, 'Don't speak that way about him. You love him.' Then she covered her mouth with her hand and apologized: 'I shouldn't have said that.'

"I looked surprised. Instantaneously, I knew Rosalie was right. I had come to love him. But he still treated me as a little sister. He did not seem to think of me in any way but that. Years went by, and I was soon eighteen. The older girls were married. One of the boys of the neighborhood asked me if I would marry him. I said, 'Yes!' though I knew I did not love him, and he was nothing like your grandfather. But I was so depressed and lonely. Mother had died by that time, so I had to tell my father. He looked surprised. 'You have thought this out well and long?'

"'No, Father, I have not.'

"'We shall see,' he said, and, of course, he talked about it to your grandfather and he, in turn, came over to me and said, 'Emily, why are you marrying that fellow? He is a boy, not yet a man.'

"I said, 'Patrick, I am marrying him because I love you, and you think I'm still a little girl. I am a grown woman, and I have wanted to be your wife for two long years now. Even my little sister knows it, and my older sister who is married and gone. She knew it too.'

"'Emily,' he said, 'it doesn't make sense. Give

me time to think.' A week went by while he and Father worked in the fields preparing for the fall harvest. Then one day he said, 'Emily, if you will tell that other fellow that your promise to him was a mistake, you and I will be married on Thanksgiving—if that is what you want.'

"We were married at St. Columkille Church in Butler City. A big crowd of people gathered. Cousin Billy Macauley was best man, my little sister the bridesmaid. Just two years later your father was born. Your grandfather wanted to name his first son after a famous priest of St. Louis, Bishop Patrick Ryan. The year we were married he became the Archbishop of Philadelphia. So we named your father Patrick Ryan Ruhane."

One of the children handed Grandma a glass of water. She drank slowly and then went on.

"Your father was entirely different from your grandfather, physically and in other ways. While grandfather was a huge, hulking man with broad but rounded shoulders, a large nose, and strong features, your father is a wiry man of moderate build, quick in movement and graceful. Your grandfather was a post oak, standing on the hill, defying blizzard and cyclone; your father is a silver maple, welcoming the spring rain and the summer sun.

"Your grandfather acted today and thought tomorrow. Your father thought today and waited overnight to act. He went to college at St. Mary's, did well in a business course, and played on the baseball team. He talked much of Father Francis Finn, who wrote stories about the school. Father

Finn did not teach him, but everyone knew of the novelist. His memory was so strong there.

"After graduating from college, your father worked on the farm for a few years. When his younger brother grew old enough to take over, Patrick Ryan Ruhane was happy enough to share the crops with him and moved into the town of St. Mary's. He worked in the office of the retail store and later at the co-op elevator.

"Your father went to Mass at the college every morning, and several of the priests thought he would go to the seminary. I'm sure he thought about it. But he was always so serious, too reserved, I thought. For him to take up an extra-serious routine of life might have been unwise. When he was forty-two years old, he married a girl of the neighborhood, Renée Ronnau. Her mother was, like me, a full-blooded member of the "True People," her father part French and part Neshnabek.

"Patrick and Renée were married at the Immaculate Conception Church in St. Mary's in 1928. When you came along, Orion, your mother wanted to name you after a star, and your father wanted you to have the same name as he, after Archbishop Patrick Ryan. Someone made the suggestion: 'Orion is a constellation, a group of stars.'

"Your father said, 'O'Ryan' means the son of Ryan.'

"So everybody was happy. And each side of the family spelled the name its own way."

IV

ORION GROWS UP

A

St. Mary's, Kansas (1944)

Orion entered St. Mary's Town High School in 1944, the fall after D-Day, the third year of the Great War. The school held classes in two buildings. In the parish building, he took his basic Latin, English, and math, and in the district school building several blocks to the west, he took his manual training and history classes and practiced basketball after school hours.

Once, there had been two schools: St. Mary's Public High School and St. Mary's Parish High School. In both schools, almost everybody was Catholic, except for the children of the few Swedish farmers. The townsfolk were all Irish or German.

The farmers in the area were Belgian or German Catholics or Swedish Lutherans.

A few winters before Orion started school, two old neighbors, a Swede and a Belgian, were having a beer after the team from the neighboring town of Wamego won the county basketball tournament.

The Swede thought out loud: "We've got to do something about our school. We can't be losing the county title every year in basketball."

"Well, I don't know what we can do," the Belgian said.

"Why don't we combine the schools?" the Swede countered. "While I'm head of the Public School Board, we could invite your institution to come freely under our authority. The School Board could rent space in the parish building from nine to three. You have better Latin and math courses over there, and we have better 'home ec' and manual training at the public building. We could have students go both places for those courses but stay where they are for the rest. We could combine sports, dramatics, and school paper. It would save the town money. You could have religion class before nine, when the building is still church property."

"I always heard you Swedes were astute politicians," the Belgian reluctantly admitted. "Well, let me tell you, I think you're a statesman. This is a wonderful idea. Let's try it."

Orion remembered that one time a syndicated writer wanted to tell the story about the unique school system that St. Mary's had developed. The mayor, who was also his father's boss at the

Farmer's Cooperative, said, "If you don't mind, don't write about our school. We don't want busybodies coming out here and interfering."

Those war years were busy and prosperous times. Orion and the rest of his classmates had plenty to do after school and on Saturdays. Many of the young men of the region had gone into active duty immediately at the start of the war. Most had joined the National Guard several years before. Few waited for the draft number to come up.

That spring, two of the boys who had still been in elementary school when Orion was in second grade died on Omaha Beach. But with the Allies advancing on all fronts, most people felt that the war would be over long before Orion and the other freshies finished school.

Orion soon learned that Latin came only with hard work. It would never come easily. His father still used his Latin Missal at Mass. So Orion approached his father one evening. "Dad, I need help with my Latin."

"I did too, when I began high school," his father said. "Your grandmother taught you your religion. But she never studied Latin. So I guess it's my task. We begin right this evening."

"Good," Orion said. "I don't want to fall behind the rest of the class."

"That makes sense, as your grandfather would say. First let me tell you why one should study Latin. It disciplines the mind, like mathematics. One has to be exact. There are no maybes. Latin clings together like the parts of a picture puzzle. It's a logical language. And we need logical people."

That began a routine of Latin tutoring every evening after the dishes were washed, dried, and replaced in the cupboard. Ryan Ruhane had always washed the dishes after dinner in the kitchen while his wife dried and they talked over the day. The children began their lessons as soon as they had cleared the table.

When Renée died and Grandmother moved in to take her place, Orion's father continued to wash the dishes while Orion and the girls dried the plates. Grandmother went into the parlor and rested for a few moments. The Rural Electrification had brought them electricity by that time. As soon as the dishes were finished, Grandmother quizzed the girls on their catechism in the front room, while his father drilled Orion on his Latin at the kitchen table.

"This will never get easy, Orion," his father said. "But life rarely gets easy. And school should get us ready for life, not for a long picnic that never comes. Plan on one hard hour of study every school night!"

While it never got easy, it had rewards. Orion first realized that he could keep up with his classmates. Later on, he was matching the brighter ones. As the school year went on, the teacher chided him less and less for being a wool gatherer.

At first he did not know what the word meant. Timidly, he asked his grandmother: "What is a wool gatherer, Grandma?"

"A dreamer, like you, son," she said. "Just make your good dreams come true!" A day or two later, when Orion came home from school, he found that his grandmother had placed a printed sign on the wall of his room: "Dream—and rise above your dreams." There it stood, alongside one she had placed there earlier. It read: "If you cannot win, make the one ahead break the record." Orion tried to do just that. Over the years, he began to realize that winning rarely stood foremost in Grandmother's mind. For him to take part, to do his best, that was what his grandmother wanted.

When the days got longer in the spring and a period of fair weather dried the fields, Ryan Ruhane said to his son: "Right after dishes, batting practice tonight."

"No Latin tonight, Dad?" Orion asked.

"Of course, Latin. After batting practice. I'll pitch to you. The girls can shag the flies in the outfield. Then they can bat." He paused. "It's nice to be able to spend a little more time with you now and then."

"Nice for us too, Dad."

"We've been so busy at the Elevator ever since the war started. Thank God it's winding down. At least in Europe."

"I heard in school today, Dad, that Kansas alone could grow enough wheat to feed the world."

"If men would put the same energy into feeding the world," his father came back, "as they have in blowing it up, we'd all get by better."

"Why can't they do that, Dad?"

"Plain, ordinary human cussedness, I guess," his father said. "I used to blame our troubles on original sin. People would laugh. So I began to say 'man's orneriness.' They'd all agree. But that's what original sin is—plain, ordinary human cussedness!"

A few evenings later Orion and boys from his class at school sat in the park talking after a softball game. Dusk was coming when one of the boys for some reason or other—or maybe no reason—opened with a loud barrage of curse words.

At that moment a man walked slowly along the sidewalk toward them. In silhouette he looked like Ryan Ruhane.

"O my God, Orion!" the loudmouthed boy blurted out. "It's your father."

The entire group froze as the man gradually came into the glare of a street light. It was not Ryan Ruhane.

"Boy, am I lucky!" the loudmouth said, with a sigh. "It's the baker. If it had been your dad, Orion, I would have felt terribly ashamed."

Orion thought, "*You should feel ashamed of your language whether my father heard you or not.*" But he felt a secret pride that his friends had such respect for his dad.

B

Post-War Kansas (1945)

The war ended the following summer, but work at the elevator continued heavy. Orion's father kept his promise to drill him daily in Latin and pitch batting practice after work in the summer months.

When fall came in his second year, Orion approached his father: "I'd like to try out for football this year."

"Football is a rugged game, son." Ryan Ruhane responded tentatively. "But if you want to try it, fine with me. When the scrimmage with older fellows gets too grueling, don't think I'll be upset if you concentrate on basketball—and your studies. Anyway, the conditioning exercise won't hurt."

"Thanks, Dad," Orion said. But he felt that his father was not happy with the idea. *Maybe I am too thin for the banging one must take.*

A week of conditioning exercise gave several of his classmates, even several juniors and seniors, the conviction that they could use the time more profitably. But Orion came back the second week. Tuesday, the team scrimmaged. Orion got in for one play. He went down under a punt. The safety caught the punt at full speed. The other end forced the runner to Orion's side of the field. Orion froze. He failed to lunge at the proper moment and awkwardly slapped at the safety as he raced by.

"I drove him to you," the other end said in anger. "You had him cornered. Why didn't you hit him?"

Orion said nothing. He knew he'd failed. *How often he lacked that instantaneous response that made others good athletes.* It was the same when he went hunting. He was the best target shooter of his age group. But when the time came to pull the trigger on a rabbit or a wild turkey, his hand did not move. *Was it instinctive, or something one could develop—that perfect timing?* That football season, he failed to survive the first cut.

When Orion mentioned this fact to his father, Ryan responded, "You tried, and that was good. My own personal feeling is that you'll do better in basketball. Your height will help there. Baseball was my best sport. I think you'll do well there, too. You have a good batting eye."

Emily Rising Moon had more to say on that matter. A few days later, when Orion came home from school, she said, "I ran into the coach's wife at the Market. She said that her husband felt that you had to put a few more pounds of muscle on those lank bones of yours to take the rugged beating that a football player takes."

Like most teenage boys, Orion hated to hear that he did not have the finest physique in town. But he knew his grandmother was right. His grandmother was a real football fan; she knew the game. Often, she'd tell about the gray oppressive day in Holy Week in 1931 when the plane that carried Notre Dame Coach Knute Rockne plunged in disaster not far from where they lived.

Many times, her grandchildren and their friends would ask her to tell them about the great football players she had seen play. Then she would respond, "Let's call a huddle," and the children would gather around her.

On one such occasion, Orion's cousin asked her, "Grandma, didn't you think Jim Thorpe was the greatest football player who ever lived?"

"Yes, I think he was. And I say that not simply because his mother was Neshnabek. Your father took me all the way to St. Louis to see him play in 1908. Saint Louis University was the best in the Middle West in those years and the Carlisle Indians among the top teams in the East. Jim Thorpe was by far the best punter until Sammy Baugh came out of Texas."

"Was Thorpe your favorite player, Grandma?"

"Not the first but the second." Grandma shook her head. "My favorite footballer was old 'Foundry John' Foley, now our assistant pastor. John Foley was twenty-four, working in a foundry in St. Louis, when he got the call to be a priest. John had little Latin. They told him to come to St. Mary's College and 'bone up' on his Latin. Well, John was a full-grown man, muscles all over. He was playing with college boys nineteen, twenty, and twenty-one. St. Mary's played Kansas State. St. Mary's made twenty-four points. That was six touchdowns in those days. Now, people will tell you that John made all six. That wasn't so. He ran the ball most of the time, but he only carried it over the goal twice in those six times. Somebody else would carry it over the goal, because all the Wildcats would be ganging up on Big John."

"Grandma," the unconvinced cousin asked once more, "was he really your favorite and not Jim Thorpe?"

"Grandson, let me repeat. Jim Thorpe was a far greater player. But I knew John Foley when he was a student. When a friend does well, we're extra happy. Your Grandfather's cousin Billy Macauley knew him from St. Louis. He introduced us. John Foley was my girlhood football hero back in the 1880s. Jim Thorpe did not play until 1908 or thereabouts."

Orion considered these stories of his grandmother as he pondered the advice she now gave. *Maybe even Jim Thorpe and Father Foley did not have the muscles to play football at my age.* He would wait and hopefully grow those needed muscles.

Orion's father often talked of enlarging their home to provide space for Grandmother's "things" stored at the ancestral home on the farm. With the war over a full year, building materials became plentiful again. Ryan Ruhane was able to make his hopes real. But in the meantime he had changed his plans. Instead of enlarging the Ruhane residence, or adding to it, Orion's father decided on a small bungalow connected to the Ruhane residence by a breezeway.

Grandmother was elated. So were the rest, especially with her front room. There she kept the things she had gathered over the years. Orion knew that his grandmother excelled in needlework. He had seen splendid skirts that she'd made years before. He had expected her "things" to be mainly examples of needlework, but the vision that welcomed him into her front room left him in awe.

When the family had traveled to Wisconsin before the war, his grandmother had purchased lovely baskets of finely woven ash. These now stood on the mantel. Graceful paintings of blue horses leaped across the wall to the right.

"Your father bought those for me on the Navajo reservation in 1926," his grandmother said. "The same Navajo young man painted all three. But other Navajo artists could have matched these. Many of their young men are excellent artists with paints and silver." She took off a bracelet and handed it to Orion. "A young man at Luckachukai near Four Corners designed this for me."

Orion had noticed many times that his grandmother wore a lovely silver bracelet. But this was the first time he looked closely at it. Simple but striking.

A carefully designed blanket hung along the

west wall of the room. His grandmother pointed to it. "We drove through a town called Two Gray Hills, south of Shiprock in that section of the Navajo Reservation that floods over into New Mexico. The town boasted the best rug maker in the entire Southwest. I have heard of no one who has challenged her. We were lucky."

"It's wonderful, Grandmother. The colors of the mockingbird—gray and black and white."

"And as beautiful as the song of the mockingbird, my grandson." She paused, reflecting, and then blurted, "Let me show you the art work I like best."

His grandmother had so many beautiful things that it made Orion feel as he had when he first went into a cafeteria in Kansas City. There were so many splendid desserts—chocolate cake, angel food, peach, apple, cherry, and coconut cream pies. He couldn't choose at the time. *And how could he now guess Grandmother's favorite treasure?*

To his surprise, she picked up a small black vase. "On the way back from the Grand Canyon," she said, "we stopped at the Pueblo village of San Ildefonso, not too far north of Santa Fe, New Mexico, just below Los Alamos, where they built the atom bomb. Julian and Maria Popavida were experimenting with black pottery. I liked it immediately and bought a vase and a saucer. The feather design was in the glaze." His grandmother handed him the vase, but Orion did not want to handle it, lest he drop it.

"Your father and I had a hunch that this would grow steadily in value. And we were right, but I think the value will rise even more amazingly in the future."

To his surprise, there was more. His grandmother showed Orion beadwork of the Arapahoe and Sioux—geometric in design—the floral pattern beadwork of the Shoshone artists, and white pottery from Acoma, the citadel on the New Mexico mesa.

"Grandmother, you have chosen the best work of all our people," Orion said in admiration.

"I tried to do that. I had hoped you would come to appreciate it. For you are the oldest, my grandson. It will all be yours someday."

"No, Grandmother, it will always be yours. Only you can know its full beauty."

C

St. Mary's High School (1946–1947)

The school hired a beautiful young lady from New Mexico to teach Spanish at the start of Orion's third year. One of the bright boys remarked: "I may not come to love the Spanish language, but I would find it easy to love a certain teacher."

Orion caught the fever. "I'd like to take Spanish as my foreign language this year, Dad, instead of Latin."

"If you want to learn Spanish also," his father countered, "that's all right with me. But you are taking four years of Latin. Don't try to weasel out of that."

"Taking two languages will be a heavy chore, Dad."

"That's probably true, Son. So give up those thoughts of Spanish for a time."

"Aw, Dad."

"No, Son. But what about this possibility? You showed me your schedule, without the Spanish. Now, if I remember correctly, the Spanish class will be held while you have a study hall period. So go to the Spanish class if you want but not for credit. If you can learn it on top of your regular lessons, fine! If not, you simply work harder."

"All right, Dad."

"This way you'll know whether you really want to learn the language or are just launching into your latest enthusiasm without asking whether or not you can carry it to the end."

The Spanish teacher proved to be as tough as she was good looking. Her assignments were rugged, her marks minimal. An *A* was an *A* with her, and nobody got one. But Orion stuck it out. He chose to stay if only to prove to his father that he could carry one of his many enthusiasms to completion. He played basketball, the sixth man who came in whenever a starter ran into foul trouble. He could put the ball into the basket from the outside consistently and helped the team win the county championship.

At the start of their fourth year, Orion's class had a new Spanish teacher, an older gentleman from Cuba. The young lady from New Mexico had gone back to Albuquerque for graduate studies. Orion went out for football again, but the coach, who also directed the basketball team, called Orion aside one day after practice.

"I want to level with you, Orion," he began. "Your best skill is catching passes. Few can touch you when you get the ball in full stride, but we have no passer. Further, we have few good seniors, but we have some speedy juniors and sophs. I plan to look to next year, to give these underclassmen lots of experience. According to my present plans, you'd get in a few games for a few minutes. I wonder if all the time you would put in would be worth it. I prefer that you concentrate on basketball. We can win the county championship again this year. Think it over."

Orion thought it over, and talked to his dad about it.

"Makes sense, son," was his father's reply.

Orion smiled. "Makes sense, Dad."

The history teacher was new too. From a little town in New York, he had gone to college in New England and came to disdain everything west of the Hudson. He thought Kansas was a mistake of the Almighty. "People were right out East when they said this was a desert," he began one day. "It was the land one went through on the way to California. No one should have stopped here. Unfortunately, they did. They should have let the redskins have it."

Orion wondered, *What is this man saying*? He looked around the room. From the expressions on their faces, several of his classmates were boiling inside but saying nothing. Orion raised his hand.

"You," the teacher said, pointing to Orion. "What's on your mind?"

"The government moved our Potawatomi

ancestors here," Orion replied. "Our people did not want to come here and did not like it at first. Things were much better back in their homelands of Indiana. But they improved this Kansas land. In time Whites wanted it. And President Lincoln decided to give it to the Whites and told our ancestors to move to Indian Territory."

"Whom are we taking about, Ruhane?" the teacher asked, perplexed. "Your ancestors? Who were these people?"

"Potawatomi," Orion came back. "They lived near the Great Lakes before the English-speaking people crossed the Appalachians. They gave the British the worst defeat they ever suffered until the Battle of the Somme." Orion really knew little about the Battle of the Somme, but his words were coming faster than his thoughts, and he recalled reading about the disaster on the Somme sometime before.

The teacher knew that he had spoken foolishly. He was not going to be a double fool like Braddock. He called a retreat. "Those are interesting observations, Ruhane," he said. "Suppose we pursue those thoughts after class. We have today's lesson to finish." He turned to the day's material.

Orion remained after class, waiting for a signal from the teacher. Several girls stayed to ask questions. When the teacher had answered these, he turned to Orion. "Where I came from we made jokes about Kansas," he said. "They were entirely out of line here."

"That's over," Orion said. "No lasting harm."

"But I want to know where we are." The teacher

replied. "Or maybe I should have said, 'Where I am!' This country is new to me. You spoke of the Potawatomi—a tribe I'm not familiar with."

"Many of us here are Potawatomi, at least in part. Both my grandmothers belonged to that tribe. Several in the class are part Potawatomi–part French and others part Irish."

"I never heard of that tribe," the teacher responded. "I'll have to get to know the territory."

"You should talk to my grandmother," Orion suggested.

"I may do just that," the teacher responded. "I'll do that this afternoon after classes if you'll introduce me." And he did just that.

D

Interlude at Oskaloosa

Orion had always preferred brunettes. One day he changed his mind. He went to a conference sponsored by the Farmers' Union. Girls from Topeka Catholic debated boys from St. Benedict's in Atchison on farm policy. A blond debater advocated Agricultural Secretary Brannan's Farm Plan in a way that made her opponents grope aimlessly. Since the debate teams sat at angles, partially facing one another, Orion had seen her at first in profile. She had seemed like a marble statue, reserved, aloof, definitely not thin but with good features. When she walked to the podium at the far end of the V-shaped arrangement, her smile captivated him. When she spoke, her voice was as golden as her hair. Her blue eyes sparkled.

"Willa Wardoner is definitely not willowy," a fellow sitting behind Orion said with a laugh. The remark annoyed Orion, but he said nothing. Suddenly, he remembered where he had seen her before, at a meeting of the Kansas State Sodality Union in Salina.

Willa spoke intelligently, convincingly. She obviously knew farm life and the needs of the farm families. She and her partner had all but clinched the debate when she made a fatal mistake. She looked at the debater on the far right. He eyed her with an expression that seemed to say, "Do you really believe what you are saying?"

His look momentarily unnerved her. She floundered for a moment, lost her train of thought. Flustered, she looked again at his vapid expression. Losing her poise, she blurted out, "Is it really that bad?"

At the end of the debate, Orion walked up to Willa. "I thought that was a lousy trick our debater pulled."

"Thank you," she said. "I should have known. I heard that he was an 'all's fair in love and war' guy." She paused.

"He is that," Orion said, then changed the subject. "How about a root beer?"

They walked from the library to the cafeteria.

"I'm Orion Ruhane from St. Mary's, Kansas," he said.

"I'm Willa Wardoner from Oskaloosa," she responded. "My mother taught school in Red

Cloud, Nebraska, where Willa Cather lived as a girl. My folks named me after her."

"I read her book, *Death Comes for the Archbishop*," Orion said.

"That's about New Mexico," Willa responded. "She wrote one about a bishop in Quebec and one about a slave-owning woman in Virginia. The rest are set in Nebraska. I hope to read all of them some day."

"I'll have to read more of her writings."

"Try *My Antonia* first."

Their friendship grew. Willa took a stiff program that did not allow a lot of free time. But they both represented their schools at the Quarterly Kansas State Sodality Union meeting. Orion began to wonder why he had never noticed her at any of the meetings before the day of the debate.

Then one day Willa called him. "I'm driving back to Oskaloosa after the next meeting. Why not come along? My folks will be happy to have you. My little sisters will like you, too. We have two fine Appaloosas. We can ride them that afternoon. I can take you to Topeka for the St. Mary's bus."

Why not? Orion thought. They had just finished mid-terms. "I'd be happy to go," he answered.

Later, he began to have second thoughts. They had known each other for such a short time. He knew so little of her parents. *How would they take him? As a friend, or a possible suitor?* She had talked of hundreds of acres of winter wheat. And she drove a car that said, "Pop is prosperous." *Wouldn't it be better to let the friendship deepen before such a visit?* But he had already said yes.

Willa drove with the throttle wide open. The road through northeast Kansas stretched before them without turn or undulation, straight as a Pawnee arrow targeting an antelope. They traveled through rich farmland with winter wheat beginning to show after the late spring snows. But they passed fewer and fewer farmhouses. "More acres in grain," Orion observed, "but fewer farmers."

"The bigger ones like my father," Willa said, "are getting bigger. The smaller farmers are moving to the cities."

"That's the way it is throughout the country."

"During my years in high school," Willa came back, "we lost two farm families each year. Yet, more land was in crops."

"The towns are getting smaller, Willa. Fewer students in school. Fewer teachers needed. One less drugstore. One less grocer."

"Thank God for Secretary Brannan," Willa said. "It's either his plan or agri-business. Even big operators like my pop will be out when the factory farms come."

"I heard you debate the Brannan Plan, Willa. And I heard Secretary Brannan himself speak. But I don't understand how his plan would work."

"You're going to hear my debate speech, again, Orion. This time, you're going to pay attention."

"I paid attention the last time, Willa. But I paid attention to you, not to what you said." He smiled.

"Shame on you, Orion. You see girls as objects, not as intelligent persons."

"I just thought you were wonderful, Willa."

"You're hopeless. But this time, you *have* to listen. We have another debate coming up. Keep quiet and listen. The big problem in rural areas is that we get lower prices for our crops, yet because of the government subsidies we overproduce."

"I'll keep quiet," Orion said.

"Here's Brannan's plan: The farmer gets what he can for his crops. That brings down the price of food for the consumer. The government will pay the difference between what the farmer got and a pre-established parity price but only for the amount of crops a family farm can produce. So the big farmers and the agri-businesses will receive no subsidies on most of their crops and instead a small portion. Without subsidies over the years they presumably will curtail their production and cut down the surplus. It's the only farm plan that aids the family farmer, lowers prices, and ends overproduction."

"Complex but clever, Willa."

"Big farmers, like my father, call Brannan a Communist." She paused then blurted out, "For God's sake, don't mention the Brannan plan to my father or that I support it."

"I won't."

So intense had been the discussion that they had failed to notice how far they had traveled. "I always feel an emptiness on these stretches," Willa said. "Willa Cather's characters feel that sense of loneliness, but in spite of it all, people like Antonia survive. I saw in a magazine article that the prototype of Antonia is still living."

"I finally got around to reading *My Antonia*,"

Orion said. "Actually, it was a history assignment. My prof wanted us to read a novel that gave the flavor of the plains—Hamlin Garland, Willa Cather, or Paul Horgan's *Whitewater*."

"You history majors are beyond hope," Willa said. "Even when you do a good thing like read literature you do it for the wrong reason."

"Wait a minute, Willa. I read one other book. *My Antonia* made me depressed, so I tried *Song of the Lark*."

"All of us in church choir think that's her best story."

"I always wanted to be able to sing, Willa, but I was never sure of my notes."

The miles rolled by. Orion felt at peace. He was at ease with Willa as he had been with no other girl except his own sisters. Maybe what he felt about Willa was brotherly. He wasn't sure, but he liked her company. And she obviously enjoyed his presence.

What of her parents? he wondered. *How would they take him? Would they look upon a visit like this as equal to an engagement? And how did Willa herself take his agreeing to come?* He should have thought of those things earlier.

"One more mile and our turnoff," she said. "We'll surprise my folks."

"Oh! Didn't you tell them that you were bringing me?"

"No, I just told them I was bringing a friend. They'll think it's a girl, as usual. But don't worry. Father will accept you because you were born on a farm. He admires our Swedish neighbors and talks a lot about them. Some think he *is* Swedish. But he's an Ulster Presbyterian and, like all Orangemen, he looks down on Irish Catholics. If he starts belittling the Green Irish, tell him about your fine Swedish neighbors in St. Mary's. Derail his remarks. Mother will like you because you're a good Catholic, so don't worry."

He did worry. But his smile won Mrs. Wardoner. Wesley Wardoner took his time to assess the visitor. His handshake was tentative.

After lunch, Wardoner asked if Orion would like to look over his spread.

"I certainly would." They walked out toward the large barn. The entire place was neat. *Just like the Swedish farmers at St. Mary's*, Orion thought. *They kept their grounds and equipment as neat as their wives kept the farm homes.*

"Great spread you have here," Orion said. "It reminds me of my grandfather's farm near St. Mary's Kansas."

"You a Jayhawker?"

"Yes I am, Mr. Wardoner."

"Your grandfather ran cattle?"

"Mostly corn and wheat. A few Herefords. Dairy cows, Holstein. But mainly he was a grain farmer."

"And what did your father do?"

"Ran the co-op Elevator for the Farmers' Union. In his spare time he managed the town credit union. An uncle ran the farm."

"I'm a Farmers' Union man myself," Wardoner came back. "But I don't like the policies of those 'Commies' in Denver who are running the central office. They thought Roosevelt was good for the country."

Orion knew it was best to close that avenue of discussion. "How many acres do you have, Mr. Wardoner?"

"Six hundred in wheat, two hundred in sorghum. We run about thirty whiteface on several acres of pasture beyond the creek."

"You have lots to be proud of, Mr. Wardoner."

"We did it ourselves. Didn't depend on government. First, we had that Henry Wallace. Now, Truman puts in that man Brannan. He wants to penalize the successful."

Orion thought back to the day he had met Willa and their conversation on the drive. She had convinced him of the wisdom of Charles Brannan's plan. He wanted to say, *Mr. Wardoner, your daughter thinks differently.* But he changed the subject. "What did you think of the choice of the new coach at Lawrence?"

"The man from Wyoming?"

"Yes."

"Can't be worse than the man we had. Oklahoma's too tough for the rest of the league. They not only have better players, they have a Swedish coach."

"Yes, that's right," Orion said.

"If a Swede is as smart as his opponent in an ordinary situation, he'll win out in tense moments. He's calmer. He can think more clearly. Last year, Colorado had much better players. But in a tense moment in a game, they were sitting on the bench. The coach was confused. The Sooners won."

"I saw the Buffaloes play Kansas in Lawrence," Orion said. "Beat them badly. But the Colorado coach left his fastest running back in the game, long after he needed him. And a big hulking Kansas tackle put the sprinter out of action for the next game with Oklahoma."

"Stupid," Wardoner said. "You can't go wrong betting on the Sooners."

They walked awhile in silence. Orion looked at all the equipment—well oiled, rust free. "Splendid equipment, Mr. Wardoner."

"I put in as much time on my tools as on my crops," Wardoner said. Then, changing the subject, he said, "Your name, Ruhane, that's Irish, isn't it?"

"Yes, it is."

"Your folks from Ireland?"

"Way back on my father's side, yes, Mr. Wardoner."

"Your mother?"

"French Canadian, from colonial days."

"Lots of French Canadians had Indian wives, didn't they?"

Willa had told him her father had a New England Puritan's dislike of Indians. *This is it. Better he should know now.* "My mother's people belonged to the Neshnabek. The French called them the Potawatomi, the People of the Fire."

"One of your grandmothers Indian?"

"Both of them!"

Wardoner stopped. His face grew tense. His features hardened. "Does my daughter know this?"

"That my grandmothers were Potawatomi?"

"Yes. Did you tell her that?"

"The subject never came up."

"I never brought my daughter up to be running around the country with redskins," Wardoner said, obviously trying to control his temper.

Orion had often heard that he might encounter such a reaction. He was ready. "My father," he came back sharply, "at no time ever thought that a son of his might number among his friends the daughter of a North-of-Ireland man."

Orion left the shocked Wardoner standing in front of the barn. In ten minutes he was out on the highway and had hitched a ride back to St. Mary's.

He had trouble getting to sleep that night. In the morning he decided to do immediately what he always did when in doubt. He talked to his grandmother.

"This is an experience I never had," she said. "The people I met knew I was a Potawatomi. You racially mixed face a different world. Like tortoises, some pull in their heads and let the armor fend off the outside world. Don't do that! Don't let the Wesley Wardoners of the world change your attitudes. 'We are all one in Christ Jesus,' St. Paul said in his day. 'Neither Roman nor Greek, slave nor free.' Neither Green nor Orange, American Indian nor White in our day."

During the next few days Orion wondered if he should phone and explain his abruptly ended visit to Oskaloosa. After all, it had been her father, not she, who had caused him to leave. She had been a good friend. In a way, he was surprised that she had not called or written a note. *But then why should she take the initiative?* He had run off. Had her father *told her what he had said?*

A friend of Willa Wardoner phoned from Topeka on Thursday. "Orion," she said, "Willa wants to talk to you. She told me what happened. She knows how you feel. It was her father's fault. She wants to tell you that. She called three times but didn't reach you."

"If she told you everything," Orion responded, "then you know I left Oskaloosa without saying goodbye to her or to her mother."

"She knows that. She understands. She wants to talk with you."

"All right," Orion said.

"She's right here," the girl said. "I'll put her on the line."

"Orion, this is Willa. I'm sorry about what my father said. I understand your feeling of not being wanted."

"I should have thanked your mother for her hospitality and you for your kindness before I headed for St. Mary's."

"My mother understood, too. Daddy has firm views, as you no doubt realized. He's taking me out of Topeka Catholic at the end of the semester. Mother insisted on a Catholic school. So they're sending me to Mount St. Scholastica in Atchison." She paused. "We will still be friends, won't we?"

"Friends, yes. Always."

E

Senior Classman

Orion's senior year proved a busy one. He had to pick up one history course and his fourth year of Latin. The fall saw a big harvest. When St. Benedict's College of Atchison came to play St. Mary's in basketball, Orion recognized several of the Ravens from Sodality meetings. One of them, a tall, broad-shouldered fellow, came up to him. "Aren't you Orion Ruhane?" he asked.

"That's right!" Orion responded.

"I'm Tom Nelson. I go with a friend of yours, Willa Wardoner. She said you were good friends when she went to Topeka Catholic."

"That we were," Orion responded. "You're a

lucky guy."

"She said you were like a brother to her, encouraging her when she lost a debate, liking the things she liked—basketball and horseback riding."

"That we were—friends. I wish both of you well."

At that moment the claxon sounded for the tip-off.

Only after that encounter did Orion realize how much the incident with Willa's father had affected him. Thank God Willa was not hurt badly. Thank God the Wesley Wardoners of the world had children who were finer human beings than they! Orion would not let the pre-judgments of others mar his life.

And what did he want from life? He had to give that question serious thought during his annual three-day retreat. Lucky for all, the retreat director was a man of extensive experience—his own pastor, Father Foley, his grandmother's favorite priest, whom she had met years before when he starred in football at St. Mary's College.

After Mass the first morning Father Foley told what all should do to make a good retreat. "Reflection . . . silence, not as a penance, but to set the stage for serious thoughts about life and its meaning. Attention! Application . . . pray mentally and orally—the Rosary, the Stations . . . above all, talk over your life problems with Jesus. . . ." The morning went quietly.

In the afternoon, the priest opened up immediately with a question: "Who was Billie Dove and who was Jim Bausch?" The retreatants looked perplexed. No one could remember having heard either name. The priest took out a ten-year-old copy of the newspaper *The Topeka Capital*. He read the predictions of immortality for the talented movie actress and the outstanding athlete of the year. Yes, immortality!! The retreat director then asked: "What doth it profit a man if he gain the whole world and suffer the loss of his own soul?"

"Achieve!" the preacher said in a voice so loud it was almost a shout. "But achieve for some lasting purpose—to help your neighbor by curing disease or spreading unselfish systems of business, or helping the downtrodden, or ending racial prejudice. Achieve by serving God as a missionary, or as an apostle to the poor, or as a teacher of truth, or as a proclaimer of God's word! Yes, *achieve*! Not for a worldly purpose but for the good of your neighbor and the cause of truth!"

"Wow," whispered a boy in the pew behind Orion, "he really laid it on the line."

On the last day of the retreat, Orion went to see Father Foley.

"I'm seriously thinking of joining the Order," Orion said.

"I presume you have thought about this a long time?"

"Off and on since my sophomore year. I knew the seminarians at the theologate. Our grade-school basketball coach was one of these. You may remember him. We called him 'Mr. Z.' His brother coached in the pros. Played at Marquette. I often thought if I could be like him. What a great life it would be! Helping people! He's up in Wyoming, working with the Arapahoe. I haven't seen him since high school days, but I always remembered him."

"Good man," Father Foley answered. "Have you told your father?"

"I told my grandmother. As you know, she's the one who counts. Father defers to her. She knew the way I was thinking. She said, 'Okay, Grandson, you're going the right way.'"

Actually, his grandmother had been a little more direct than usual. "Did the affair at Oskaloosa have anything to do with this decision?" she had asked.

"I don't think so, Grandmother. I liked Willa a lot. Maybe I would have come to love her. That's over, with no hurt."

"Good. You will probably fall in love, or think you have fallen in love, many times. And many more girls and their mothers will think they are in love with you. Can you live in the midst of married people and give up the possibility of a life companion of your own and the possibility of children?"

"I think I can, Grandmother."

"The first two years are a trial time, I understand," Grandmother went on. "One may leave any time during those early months. If you do decide that the religious routines of life are not for you, leave—and don't look back. Don't be half in, half out the rest of your life."

"I'll try, Grandmother."

"When you go, keep the image of the great priests who helped our people—Father Christian

Hoecken, Father Benjamin Petit, Father Maurice Gailland, and the others."

"I'll try, Grandmother, to be generous as they were."

"I think, Grandson, you will stick to your goal."

V

DIFFERENT HORIZON

A Birthplace of the Blackrobes

After graduation, Orion spent the summer working at the co-op elevator. When he told his father about his plans for the fall, Ryan Ruhane said simply, "As long as it's not the Trappists or the diocesan seminary, it's okay with me. I know you talked to your grandmother."

Orion realized instinctively that he did not have a Trappist vocation. Too many hours of silence. Too rugged a regime of prayer and fasting. Especially prayer at odd hours of the night. Only later did he come to realize the wisdom of his father's other caution. Orion needed the structure a religious rule required.

September was soon at hand. His father had planned to drive him to the seminary near St. Louis. But August had seen rain that year and the crops were coming into the co-op early. Ryan could not get away. He drove Orion into Topeka for the early morning train that had not stopped at St. Mary's. It reached St. Louis about noon.

The Director had written directions. Orion was to take a cab or a Forest Park streetcar that ran west from the Union Station and passed two blocks from Saint Louis University. A seminarian would meet him at the door of the Faculty Residence and take him to lunch.

By one o'clock the two of them were on their way to Florissant, a suburb twenty miles northwest of the heart of the city. One of the Jesuits he had consulted about going to the novitiate suggested that he spend his last dollars on malted milks for himself and his companion.

"No time," the driver said. "We're due at the novitiate at two." Orion wondered why the great hurry but said nothing. He really would have liked to have one more thick malted.

The seminary stood on a ridge overlooking the richest farmland in the entire state of Missouri. The French colonial pioneers called it "Florissant," flourishing. Brick buildings clustered around a stately white stone structure.

The Historical Association of St. Louis County had set up a historical marker that told its story: "St. Stanislaus, the oldest Jesuit seminary in continued existence anywhere in the world, stemmed from the vision and effort of four men.

President James Monroe offered a subsidy to any group with a workable plan to aid the Indians. Bishop Louis W. V. DuBourg of Louisiana Territory planned a combined Indian School and clerical seminary on these fertile acres. Father Charles Felix Van Quickenborne brought a group of Belgian Jesuit recruits to staff the school. General William Clark, Indian Commissioner, approved the plan. Sauk and Iowa boys came in 1824, and later Osage."

In a briefing that evening with other newcomers, Orion learned that the Indian School had lasted only a few years, but the clerical seminary flourished. Its graduates founded high schools, colleges, parishes, and universities throughout the Midwest. They began missions among his people—the Osage, the Salish, the Sioux, and the Arapahoe. The most famous alumni were missionaries Peter Jan De Smet and Maurice Gailland, juvenile novelist Francis Finn, and educators Peter Verhaegen, William Banks Rogers, and Sodality promoter Daniel Lord.

"What a story!" Orion thought.

During the next few days, Orion and the other novices soon learned that the silence at St. Stanislaus Seminary was as strict as that of the Trappists, except for a half hour after dinner and supper. Only on feasts did the novices meet with third- and fourth-year men, called juniors.

When Orion arrived in 1952 the seminary had a faculty of fifteen priests and a student body of 160, with about forty in each class. Each seminarian had before him two years of spiritual instruction.

During this time he could leave at any point. After that, he would take his vows of poverty, chastity, and obedience for life. Then he had two years of classical studies.

The two groups lived in identical buildings. Between them stood a taller building that housed an auditorium in the basement, dining hall on the first floor, and chapel on the top floor. This complex stood behind the Rock Building that housed the administration and dated back to the 1840s.

The daily schedule smacked of a barracks more than a boarding school, although it had elements of both. Prayer matched silence with an endless repetition of minor duties, little variety, and total stability. The city of St. Louis, twenty miles away, might as well have been in western Kansas. No slipping into town for a Cardinal baseball game or a John Wayne movie. No radio. No one even thought of TV, just making its debut.

The silence and continual round of duties would never get easy—but these hit him slowly. After a week of introduction, on a special feast day each received the traditional black robe of the Jesuit order. That year the Supervisor chose the late September Feast of the North American Martyrs, the eight French Jesuits whom the Iroquois had killed back in colonial days.

The regimentation rivaled a Prussian barracks. The head novice read off the names of the two companions one was to walk with on Sunday and Tuesday afternoons, the work teams, and the after-meals crews for dining hall or scullery. Only on Thursday afternoons did the novices play baseball or basketball outside, depending on the season.

From five in the morning until nine at night, the schedule called for a round of minor duties that seemed to add up to nothing. The religious instructions sailed as high over Orion's head as the planes taking off for Chicago from Lambert International a few miles away. "The Director speaks in calculus," a fellow novice remarked one day. "I'm still struggling with algebra."

The priest who came for the annual community retreat was more down to earth. Orion listened attentively. The retreat master praised a book by Johannes Lindworsky, a German Jesuit who had died in a concentration camp during World War II. While so many retreat directors concentrated on the practice of virtues, Father Lindworsky urged the development of a vocational ideal. The retreatant was to ask himself what he wanted to accomplish in his priestly life, and then, with the approval of his superior, was to keep moving toward that goal.

Orion wanted to teach people the history of the Church, to strengthen the faith of his fellow Catholics, and to point out to the "Separated Brothers" why their leaders had severed ties with Mother Church.

Orion told the retreat director of his hoped-for path.

"Good" was the response. "Point your every action to that goal."

Orion felt he had taken a major step forward with his "vocational ideal."

Christmas came, a glorious time. Orion realized that he had never really appreciated Christmas before. A card from his father cut the joy. His grandmother had taken ill. After that, Lent proved grim. And the summer reminded Orion of his home area of Kansas. But the fall outranked any he had met, with a walkway of sugar maples, their leaves aglow with the color of ripened pears.

Shortly after his second Christmas at St. Stanislaus, sad news came. His grandmother's condition grew serious. The rule of the novitiate did not allow novices to attend funerals other than that of mother and father. But the Father Rector at the St. Mary's School of Theology had called the Master of Novices and assured him that Emily Rising Moon had taken the place of Orion's mother. Orion arrived in St. Mary's shortly before she died.

The Topeka Capital carried her obituary, an unusually long one. "Pioneer Kansas Woman Passes," the headline read. "Emily Rising Moon (Mrs. Patrick Sarsfield Ruhane), daughter of Neosho Rising Moon, who came to Kansas with the first contingent of the Potawatomi tribe before the Civil War, herself a leader in tribal and religious activities for many years, passed away quietly at her home near St. Mary's, Thursday last. The Rev. John Foley, S.J., associate pastor at the Immaculate Conception Church in St. Mary's, and a friend of the Ruhanes since his college days in St. Mary's, gave the last rites of the Catholic Church. Two sons, seven grandchildren, and ten great-grandchildren survive her.

"The funeral Mass will be at 10 a.m., Thursday, Jan. 26, at St. Mary's. Father Foley will conduct the ceremony and give a eulogy. A large crowd is expected, especially members of the various Catholic sodalities and of Indian organizations. Representatives of several Oklahoma tribes and Potawatomi relatives from there and from Wisconsin and Michigan are expected to attend."

The January thaw held for the funeral. In his remarks at the funeral Mass, Father Foley offered a few words of comment on the scriptural readings of the day and then reminisced about his own friendship with the deceased.

"I knew Billy Macauley, the cousin and partner of the man Emily Rising Moon married, before they came out from St. Louis to farm with 'Father Butler's Boys,' the Irish lads who settled at Blaine, then called Butler City. I met Emily, her father, and her future husband, Patrick Ruhane, with my friend Billy, after a football game. Billy Macauley brought them to meet me. Emily was a great fan, but not her husband. She had to drag him to the games.

"The following year I entered the Jesuit novitiate at Florissant and did not see them until I returned as assistant pastor after ordination. But we kept in touch.

"Emily was the ridgepole for all her descendants and especially for her son Patrick Ryan Ruhane's family after her daughter-in-law died. She was the one who taught the children to live their faith, to keep their minds on Jesus Christ, and live His way. A great storyteller, she recounted the legends of her people, the Neshnabek, the 'True People' she called them, and all her offspring were true people, true to God, true to country, true to their families, and true to themselves. May God send us more like her. Amen."

The Archbishop of Kansas City in Kansas sat in the sanctuary and gave the final commendation.

Orion felt as if an awesome wind out of the past had uprooted the ancient oak from the Ruhane's front yard and swept it a mile into the Kaw River. But he had an unforgettable memory to carry him on: His grandmother said he'd persevere. And he knew she was always right.

Author's Note

All the Potawatomi in Emily Rising Moon's narration and all her Irish relations are fictional. The events she relates, however, are factual. Records affirm them.

While history remembers Fathers Marquette and Allouez of colonial times, it has until recently overlooked Father Benjamin Petit of early American days.

Father Ambrose Butler, a priest of the Archdiocese of St. Louis, did promote a successful Irish colony in Kansas, as Emily assures us, and football star John Foley returned to St. Mary's after his ordination to the priesthood to serve as assistant pastor at Immaculate Conception Church.